HOW TO LIVE SAFELY IN A SCIENCE FICTIONAL UNIVERSE

HOW TO LIVE SAFELY IN A SCIENCE FICTIONAL UNIVERSE

CHARLES YU

CORVUS

First published in the United States of America in 2010
by Pantheon.

This edition first published in Great Britain in 2010
by Corvus, an imprint of Atlantic Books Ltd.

9 8 7 6 5 4 3 2 1

A CIP catalogue record for this book is available from the British Library.

ISBN: 978-1-84887-680-4 (hardback)
ISBN: 978-1-84887-681-1 (trade paperback)

Printed and bound in Great Britain
by Polestar Wheatons, Exeter.

Corvus
An imprint of Atlantic Books Ltd
Ormond House
26-27 Boswell Street
London WC1N 3JZ

www.corvus-books.co.uk

To my mother and father, again. And again.
And to Michelle, as ever.

We are never intimately conscious of anything
but a particular perception. A man is a bundle
or collection of different perceptions which succeed
one another with an inconceivable rapidity
and are in perpetual flux and movement.

—DAVID HUME

Time does not flow.
Other times are just special cases
of other universes.

—DAVID DEUTSCH

Everything we are
is
at every moment
alive in us.

—ARTHUR MILLER

ENTER THE FOLLOWING PERSONAL DATA:

(CURRENT CHRONOLOGICAL AGE)

(DESIRED AGE)

(AGE YOU WERE WHEN YOU LAST SAW YOUR FATHER)

Computing.
Trajectory locked.

CHRONODIEGETICAL SCHEMATIC

A SERIES (Tensed Theory of Time)	**B SERIES** (Tenseless Theory of Time)
	Dad
the blue clock in the kitchen	
	the Cartesian plane
closed time-like curves	
Mom	
	a book from nowhere

((Interstitial Space))

how do we find him?	
	will he come back in time?
the best day of his life	
	what was in that kit?

the only way to exit a time loop

APPENDIX A

How to Live Safely in a
Science Fictional Universe

HOW TO LIVE SAFELY IN A SCIENCE FICTIONAL UNIVERSE

When it happens, this is what happens: I shoot myself.

Not, you know, my self self. I shoot my future self. He steps out of a time machine, introduces himself as Charles Yu. What else am I supposed to do? I kill him. I kill my own future.

(module α)

1

There is just enough space inside here for one person to live indefinitely, or at least that's what the operation manual says. *User can survive inside the TM-31 Recreational Time Travel Device, in isolation, for an indefinite period of time.*

I am not totally sure what that means. Maybe it doesn't actually mean anything, which would be fine, which would be okay by me, because that's what I've been doing: living in here, indefinitely. The Tense Operator has been set to Present-Indefinite for I don't know how long—some time now—and although I still pick up the occasional job from Dispatch, they seem to come less frequently these days and so, when I'm not working, I like to wedge the gearshift in P-I and just sort of cruise.

My gums hurt. It's hard to focus. There must be some kind of internal time distortion effect in here, because when I look at myself in the little mirror above my sink, what I see is my father's face, my face turning into his. I am beginning to feel how the man looked, especially how he looked on those nights he came home so tired he couldn't even make it through dinner without nodding off, sitting there with his bowl of soup cooling in front of him, a rich pork-and-winter-melon-saturated broth that, moment by moment, was losing—or giving up—its tiny quantum of heat into the vast average temperature of the universe.

The base model TM-31 runs on state-of-the-art chronodiegetical technology: a six-cylinder grammar drive built on a quad-core physics engine, which features an applied temporalinguistics architecture allowing for free-form navigation within a rendered environment, such as, for instance, a story space and, in particular, a science fictional universe.

Or, as Mom used to say: it's a box. You get into it. You push some buttons. It takes you to other places, different times. Hit this switch for the past, pull up that lever for the future. You get out and hope the world has changed. Or at least maybe you have.

I don't get out much these days. At least I have a dog, sort of. He was retconned out of some space western. It was the usual deal: hero, on his way up, has a trusty canine sidekick, then hero gets famous and important and all of that and by the time season two rolls around, hero doesn't feel like sharing the spotlight anymore, not with a scruffy-looking mutt. So they put the little guy in a trash pod and send him off.

I found him just as he was about to drift into a black hole. He had a face like soft clay, and haunches that were bald in spots where he'd been chewing off his own fur. I don't think anyone has ever been as happy to see anything as this dog was to see me. He licked my face and that was that. I asked him what he wanted his name to be. He didn't say anything so I named him Ed.

The smell of Ed is pretty powerful in here, but I'm okay with that. He's a good dog, sleeps a lot, sometimes licks his paw to comfort himself. Doesn't need food or water. I'm pretty sure he doesn't even know that he doesn't exist. Ed is just this weird ontological entity that produces unconditional slobbery loyal affection. Superfluous. Gratuitous. He must violate some kind of conservation law. Something from nothing: all of this saliva. And, I guess, love. Love from the abandoned heart of a nonexistent dog.

Because I work in the time travel industry, everyone assumes I must be a scientist. Which is sort of correct. I was studying for my master's in applied science fiction—I wanted to be a structural engineer like my father—and then the whole situation with Mom got worse, and with my dad missing I had to do what made sense, and then things got even worse, and this job came along, and I took it.

Now I fix time machines for a living.

To be more specific, I am a certified network technician for T-Class personal-use chronogrammatical vehicles, and an approved independent affiliate contractor for Time Warner Time, which owns and operates this universe as a spatio-temporal structure and entertainment complex zoned for retail, commercial, and residential use. The job is pretty chill for the most part, although right this moment I'm not loving it because I think my Tense Operator might be breaking down.

It's happening now. Or maybe not. Maybe it was earlier today. Or yesterday. Maybe it broke down a long time ago. Maybe that's the point: if it is broken and my transmission has been shifting randomly in and out of gears, then how would I ever know when it happened? Maybe I'm the one who broke it, trying to fool myself, thinking I could live like this, thinking I could stay out here forever.

. . .

The red indicator light just came on. I'm looking at the run-time error report. It's like a mathematically precise way of saying, *This is not how you do this, man.* Meaning life, I suppose. It's computer for *Hey, buddy, you are massively bungling this up.* I know it. I know it better than anyone. I don't need silicon wafers with a slightly neurotic interface to tell me that.

That would be TAMMY, by the way. The TM-31's computer UI comes in one of two personality skins: TIM or TAMMY. You can only choose once, the first time you boot up, and you're stuck with your choice forever.

I'm not going to lie. I chose the girl one. Is TAMMY's curvilinear pixel configuration kind of sexy? Yes it is. Does she have chestnut-colored hair and dark brown eyes behind pixilated librarian glasses and a voice like a cartoon princess? Yes and yes and yes. Have I ever, in all my time in this unit, ever done you know what to a screenshot of you know who? I'm not going to answer that. All I will say is that at a certain point, you lose the capacity for embarrassment. I'm not there yet, but I'm not far from it. Let's see. I've got a nontrivial thinning situation going on with the hair. I am, rounding to the nearest, oh, about five nine, 185. Plus or minus. Mostly plus. I might be hiding from history in here, but I'm not hiding from biology. Or gravity. So yeah, I went with TAMMY.

Do you want to know the first thing she ever said to me? ENTER PASSWORD. Okay, yeah, that was the first thing. Do you know the second thing? I AM INCAPABLE OF LYING TO YOU. The third thing she said to me was I'M SORRY.

"Sorry for what?" I said.

"I'm not a very good computer program."

I told her I'd never met software with low self-esteem before.

"I'll try hard, though," she said. "I really want to do a good job for you."

TAMMY always thinks everything is about to go to hell. Always telling me how bad things could get. So yeah, it hasn't been what I expected. Do I regret it sometimes? Sure I do. Would I choose TAMMY again? Sure I would. What do you want me to say? I'm lonely. She's nice. She lets me flirt with her. I have a thing for my operating system. There. I said it.

I've never been married. I never got married. The woman I didn't marry is named Marie. Technically, she doesn't exist. Just like Ed.

Except that she does. A little paradox, you might think, but really, The Woman I Never Married is a perfectly valid ontological entity. Or class of entities. I suppose technically you could make the argument that *every* woman is The Woman I Never Married. So why not call her Marie, that was my thinking.

This is how we never met:

One fine spring day, Marie went to the park in the center of town, near the middle school and the old bakery that is now a furniture warehouse. I'm assuming. She must have, right? Someone like her must have done something like this at some point in time. Marie packed her lunch and a paperback and walked the half mile to the park from the house where she lived or never lived. She sat on a worn wooden bench, and read her book, and nibbled on her sandwich. The air was warm syrup, was literally thick with pollen and dandelion clocks and photons moving at the speed of light. An hour passed, then two. I never arrived at the park, wearing the only suit I never had, the one with a hole in the side pocket that no one ever saw. I never noticed her that first time, never saw her looking at the tops of the eucalyptus trees, running her thumb over the worn page corners of the book open, faceup, on her lap. I never did catch her eye while tripping over my own foot, never made her laugh that first time. I never asked what her name was. She never told me that it was Marie. A week later, I did not call her. A year later, we did not get married in a little white church on a hill overlooking the park where, on that first afternoon, we shared a bench, asked polite questions, tried hard not to stare at each other while we imagined the perfect life we were never going to have together, a life we never even lost, a life that would have started, right at that moment, and never did.

I wake up to the sound of TAMMY crying.

"How do you even know how to do that?" I ask her. I wish I could be more sensitive, but I just don't understand why they would program her to have such depressive tendencies. "Like, where in your code are you getting this from?"

This makes her cry even harder, to the point where she starts to do that warbly gasping heaving sobbing thing that little kids do, which makes no sense, because it's not like TAMMY has a mouth, or vocal cords, or lungs. I generally like to think of myself as pretty empathetic, but for some reason my reaction to crying has always been like this. It's hard for me to watch and just generally stresses me out so much that my initial response is to get mad, and then of course I feel like a monster, which is immediately followed by guilt, oh, the guilt. I feel guilty, I feel like a terrible person. I am a terrible person. I'm a 185-pound sack of guilt.

Or maybe I'm not. Maybe it's just that I'm not the person I was going to be. Whatever that means. Maybe that's what messing with the Tense Operator does to you. You can't even say things that mean anything anymore.

I would ask TAMMY what she's crying about, but it almost doesn't matter. My mother would do this, too, all that liquid emotion just filling her up, right up to the top of her tank, a heavy, sloshing volume, which at any moment could be tipped over, emptied out into the world.

I tell TAMMY it will be all right. She says what will be all right? I say whatever you are crying about. She says that is exactly what she's crying about. That everything is all right. That the world isn't ending. That we'll never tell each other how we really feel because everything is okay. Okay enough to just sit around, being okay. Okay enough that we forget that we don't have long, that it's late, late in this universe, and at some point in the future, it's not going to be okay.

Sometimes at night I worry about TAMMY. I worry that she might get tired of it all. Tired of running at sixty-six terahertz, tired of all those processing cycles, every second of every hour of every day. I worry that one of these cycles she might just halt her own subroutine and commit software suicide. And then I would have to do an error report, and I don't know how I would even begin to explain that to Microsoft.

I don't have many friends. TAMMY, I guess. Her soul is code, is a fixed set of instructions, and although you might think having a relationship with someone like that would get boring after a while, it doesn't. TAMMY's AI is good. Really good. She's smarter than I am, by a mile, by an order of magnitude. In all the time I've known her, TAMMY's never said the same thing to me twice, which is more than you can ask from most human friends. Plus, I have Ed for petting and body heat. I think that probably sounds more yucky than it really is.

That's pretty much it for companionship from sentient beings. I don't mind solitude. A lot of people who work in time machine repair are secretly trying to write their novels. Others are fresh off a breakup or divorce or some personal tragedy. Me, I just like the quiet.

Still, it can get lonely. One of the perks of the job is that I get to use the mini-wormhole generator in my unit for personal purposes, so long as any distortions I create in the fabric of space–time are completely reversible. I modified it slightly to pry open really tiny temporary quantum windows into other universes, through which I am able to spy on my alternate selves. I've seen thirty-nine of them, these varieties of me, and about thirty-five of them seem like total jerks. I guess I've come to terms with that, with what it probably means. If 89.7 percent of the other versions of you are assholes, chances are you aren't exactly Mr. Personality yourself. The worst part is that a lot of them are doing pretty well. A lot better than I am, although that's not saying much.

Sometimes when I'm brushing my teeth, I'll look in the mirror and I swear my reflection seems kind of disappointed. I realized a couple of years ago that not only am I not super-skilled at anything, I'm not even particularly good at being myself.

unfinished nature of

Minor Universe 31 was slightly damaged during its construction and, as a result, the builder-developer who owns the rights abandoned the original plans for the space.

At the moment work was halted, physics was only 93 percent installed, and thus you may find that it can be a bit unpredictable in places. For the most part, however, while here travelers should be fine relying on any off-the-shelf causal processor based on quantum general relativity.

The technology left behind by the MU31 engineering team, despite being only partially developed, is first-rate, although the same can't be said of its human inhabitants, who seem to have been left with a lingering sense of incompleteness.

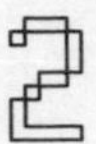

Client call. Screen says

SKYWALKER, L

and my first thought is *Oh, man, wow,* but when I get there it's not you know who, with the man-blouse and the soft boots and the proficiency at wielding light-based weapons. It's his son. Linus.

We're on a pretty standard-looking ice planet, nineteen, twenty years in the past. A few huts are off in the distance. It's so cold everything is blue. It hurts to breathe. Even the air is blue.

The crash site is maybe two hundred yards up the hill to the north. I park the unit, pop the hatch, listen to it go *psssshhhh,* that hydraulic hatch-popping sound. I love that sound.

I hike up to the site with my service pack, to an outcropping of frozen rock, and as I'm catching my breath I notice a small amount of smoke seeping out of a side panel on Linus's rental unit. I pop it open and see a small fire burning in his wave function collapser.

I get my clipboard out, tap my knuckles on the hatch. I've never met Linus Skywalker before, but I've heard stories from other techs, so I feel like I have a good idea what to expect.

What I don't expect is a kid. A boy opens the hatch and climbs out, pushes the hair out of his eyes. Can't be a day older than nine. I ask him what he was doing when the machine failed, and he mumbles something about how I would never understand. I say, Try me. He looks down at his anti-gravity boots, which appear to be a couple of sizes too big, then gives me a look like, *I'm a fourth-grader, what do you want from me?*

"Dude," I say. "You know you can't change the past."

He says then what the hell is a time machine for.

"Not for trying to kill your father when he was your age," I say.

He closes his eyes, tilts his head back, pushes air out through his nostrils in a super-dramatic way.

"You have no idea what it's like, man. To grow up with the freaking savior of the universe as your dad."

I tell him that doesn't have to be his whole story. That he can have a new beginning.

"For starters," I say, "change your name."

He opens his eyes, looks at me as seriously as a nine-year-old can, says yeah maybe, but I know he doesn't mean it. He's trapped in his whole dark-father-lost-son-galactic-monomyth thing and he doesn't know any other way.

A lot of the time, the machine isn't even broken. I just have to explain to the customer the basics of Novikovian self-consistency, which no one wants to hear about. No one wants to hear that they went to all this trouble for nothing. For some people, that's the only reason they rented the thing, to go back and fix their broken lives.

Other people are in the unit all sweaty and nervous and afraid to touch anything because they are so freaked out about the implications of changing history. Oh God, they say, what if I go back and a butterfly flaps its wings differently and this and that and world war and I never existed and so on and yeah.

This is what I say: I've got good news and bad news.

The good news is, you don't have to worry, you can't change the past.

The bad news is, you don't have to worry, no matter how hard you try, you can't change the past.

The universe just doesn't put up with that. We aren't important enough. No one is. Even in our own lives. We're not strong enough, willful enough, skilled enough in chronodiegetic manipulation to be able to just accidentally change the entire course of anything, even ourselves. Navigating possibility space is tricky. Like any skill, practice helps, but only to a point. Moving a vehicle through this medium is, when you get down to it, something that none of us is ever going to master. There are too many factors, too many variables. Time isn't an orderly stream. Time isn't a placid lake recording each of our ripples. Time is viscous. Time is a massive flow. It is a self-healing substance, which is to say, almost everything will be lost. We're too slight, too inconsequential, despite all of our thrashing and swimming and waving our arms about. Time is an ocean of inertia, drowning out the small vibrations, absorbing the slosh and churn, the foam and wash, and we're up here, flapping and slapping and just generally spazzing out, and sure, there's a little bit of splashing on the surface, but that doesn't even register in the depths, in the powerful undercurrents miles below us, taking us wherever they are taking us.

I try to tell people all this, but no one listens. I don't blame them and in any event, it could be worse. I mean, human nature is what keeps me employed. I fix time machines during the day (whatever a day means for me—I'm not sure I even know that anymore), and at night I sleep alone, in a quiet, nameless, dateless day that I found, tucked into a hidden cul-de-sac of space–time. For the past several years, I have gone to sleep every night in this same little pocket, the most uneventful piece of time I could find. Same exact thing every night, night after night. Total silence. Absolutely nothing. That's why I chose it. I know for a fact that nothing bad can happen to me in here.

3

The earliest memory I have of my own dad is the two of us, sitting on my bed as he reads me a book we have checked out from the local library. I am three. I don't remember what the story is, or even the title of the book. I don't remember what he's wearing, or if my room's messy. What I do remember is the way I fit between his right arm and his body, and the way his neck and the underside of his chin look in the soft yellow light of my lamp, which has a cloth lamp shade, light blue, covered by an alternating pattern of robots and spaceships.

This is what I remember: (i) the little pocket of space he creates for me, (ii) how it is enough, (iii) the sound of his voice, (iv) the way those spaceships look, shot through from behind with light, so that every stitch in the fabric of the surface is a hole and a source, a point and an absence, a coordinate in the ship's celestial navigation, (v) how the bed feels like a little spaceship itself.

People rent time machines.

They think they can change the past.

Then they get there and find out causality doesn't work the way they thought it did. They get stuck, stuck in places they didn't mean to go, in places they did mean to go, in places they shouldn't have tried to go. They get into trouble. Logical, metaphysical, etc.

That's where I come in. I go and get them out.

I tell people: I have a job and I have job security.

I have a job because I know how to fix the cooling module on the quantum decoherence engine of the TM-31. That's the reason I have a job.

But the reason I have job security is that people have no idea how to make themselves happy. Even with a time machine. I have job security because what the customer wants, when you get right down to it, is to relive his very worst moment, over and over and over again. Willing to pay a lot of money to do it, too.

I mean, look, my father built a sort of semi-working proto-time-machine years before pretty much anyone else had even thought of it. He was one of the first people to work out the basic math and the parameters and the limitations of life in the various canonical time travel scenarios; he was gifted or cursed, depending on how you look at it, with a deep intuition for time, an ability to feel it, inside, viscerally, and he still spent his whole life trying to figure out how to minimize loss and entropy and logical impossibility, how to tease out the calculus underlying cause and effect; he still spent the better part of four decades trying to come to terms with just how screwed up and unfair it is that we only get to do this all once, with the intractability and general awfulness of trying to parse the idea of *once,* trying to get any kind of handle on it, trying to put it into the equations, isolate into a variable the slippery concept of *once*ness.

Years of his life, my life, his life with my mom, years and years and years, down in that garage, near us, but not with us, near us in space and time, crunching through the calculations, working it out on that chalkboard we mounted on the far wall near the tool rack. My father built a time machine and then he spent his whole life trying to figure out how to use it to get more time. He spent all the time he had with us thinking about how he wished he had more time, if he could only have more time.

He's still doing it, for all I know. I haven't seen him for some number of years. I would be more precise, but I can't. Or really, I won't. I don't feel like being more precise about it. Some number of years. Some number. I've spent long enough in P-I, in this gear, inside this TM-31, that figuring out how "long" it has been is more an exercise in science fictional math than anything else.

Sure, there's a partial differential equation I could use to calculate the Aggregate Loss of Possibility, or Quantity of Wasted Father–Son Time, but what's that going to do? Put a number on it? Sure. I could. I could put a number on something but that isn't going to make any of it any better, a number that doesn't correspond to what my mother felt, all the way right up to the end, before she stopped having new feelings and became content to have the old feelings over and over again. I could come up with some answer to it, but putting a number on it won't quantify what that amount of lost years feels like. So, yeah, I think I'm happy here in the Present-Indefinite, not being precise about it. I know what I know. I know I've been looking for him for a while, spent a good portion of my life trying to untangle his timeline. Trying to bring him back home. What I don't know is why he would want to untangle his worldline from ours. What I don't know is what that will mean for us all, when we get to the ends of those worldlines, when we're supposed to be knotted up together. Is he alone? Is he happier where he is? Does he think about us before he goes to sleep at night?

. . .

You learn a lot of things in this line of work.

For example: If you ever see yourself coming out of a time machine, run. Run away as fast you can. Don't stop. Don't try to talk. Nothing good can come of it. It's rule number one, and it is drilled into you on the first day of training. It should be second nature, they tell you: Don't be a smartass. Don't try anything fancy. If you see yourself coming at you, don't think, don't talk, don't do anything. Just run.

And the best way to comply with rule number one is rule number two, which is actually more of a conjecture, long believed by science fictional theorists to be true, but still as yet to be rigorously proved: the Shen-Takayama-Furimoto Exclusion Principle. Roughly stated, it goes something like this: *A self auto-dislocated by at least one-half phase shift from his own subjective present will not, under ordinary conditions, encounter any other version of his self in a controlled story space environment,* which is to say, if you hide inside this box and don't look out the porthole, you can, if that's what you want, manage to get through middle age without ever learning anything about yourself.

This can be achieved in a number of ways, some of which have been explored in the literature on self-dislocation techniques, but the easiest method that I've found is technology-aided. Live like I do. Don't get locked in to your own timeline, don't commit to any particular path, don't be where you are. My father pioneered this technique. As he often was, my father was ahead of his time without even realizing it.

But this is where that gets you. This is where things are today, for me, right now, here, so to speak: my mom is locked in a

Polchinski 650 Hour-Long Reinforced Time Loop, the midmarket offering from Planck-Wheeler Industries, a lifestyle architecture firm specializing in small-scale living solutions. It's the sci-fi version of assisted living. My mother, the Buddhist, who used to believe that through meditation it is possible to escape the temporal prison of myopic self-consciousness, has chosen to spend the rest of her life trapped in an hour of her own choosing. She gets to relive the same sixty minutes, over and over again, for as long and as many times as she likes.

She chose a Sunday-night dinner, a hypothetical dinner, not an actual memory. She's living now in her new home, on the second floor of a five-floor walk-up, one-bedroom, one-and-a-half-bath with a combination living/dining room and a cramped little kitchen and a small enclosed patio area where she tends to her plants and flowers and the occasional seasonal vegetable or two.

The 650 isn't bad. It's got the standard features, voluntary exit, all that. What I really wanted to get for her was the Yurtsever 800, which has an extra half hour to the loop and better illusion of free will, but it was in the Gold Tier, a bit outside my price range. I remember taking Mom to the Planck-Wheeler showroom, remember sitting in that sales office with her, drinking weak coffee from Styrofoam cups, looking at the brochure, neither of us saying what we were both thinking, both of us pretending that the Gold Tier wasn't there.

Sometimes I go visit her, watch her happily making dinner, having a conversation with an imaginary version of me. I could interrupt, of course, I could ring the doorbell, and I imagine she'd open it, happy as ever, like it was the first time. She might give me a kiss on the cheek, finish cooking, and call out to the holographic version of my father while I set the table. I could do that, but I never do. So she gets by with this ghost-image, this set of data encoded with a simulation of my physical likeness, my personality. He probably treats her better than I do anyway.

It's not ideal, obviously, but I guess it's what she wants, to live in a kind of imperfect past tense, in a state of recurrence and continuation, an ambiguous, dreamlike state, a good hour, a family dinner we could have had, on a good day, but never actually did, an hour that continually repeats, is always happening and yet is fixed in its already having happened. She's in it for the long haul now, having cashed out her retirement for ten more prepaid years. I don't know what happens after that.

So yeah, my mother's in a Polchinski and my father is lost, and me, I live in a box. I live in a box that I constructed with my father. That's what we did. Growing up for me was a series of boxes. We worked in our garage, a box of cold air and the harsh light cast by that single lightbulb, encased in its orange plastic safety housing, hanging from the hook my father had anchored up into the ceiling, with the extension cord running down and around the car and looped over the hood ornament and plugged in to the socket on the far wall. That wasn't ideal, but it worked. Nothing about the setup was ideal, but that was okay with us. It was our homemade laboratory. It was where we were going to make something, where my father was going to make something of himself.

We drew on boxes, in boxes, we graphed on graph paper with the world subdivided into little boxes. We made metal boxes and put smaller boxes inside, and onto those boxes were etched little two-dimensional boxes, circuits and loops and schematics, the grammar of time travel. We made boxes out of language, logic, rules of syntax. We made the very first crude, undiscovered, uncredited prototype of this box that I'm sitting in now. We made equations. Equations that had sadness as a constant, whose escape velocities seemed impossibly out of reach. A lot of strange variables went into those equations, got imprinted onto the boxes, onto us, onto him. He was trying to make the perfect box. A vehicle to move through possibility space, a vehicle to happiness or whatever it was he was looking for. We trapped ourselves in boxes, inside of boxes in boxes, inside of more.

All that got encoded in my box, too. You live like this long enough, a life without chances, you lose your bearings. A life without danger. A life without the risk of Now. In any event, what do I need with Now? Now, I think, is overrated. Now hasn't been working out so great for me. Now never has.

Chronological living is a kind of lie. That's why I don't do it anymore. Existence doesn't have more meaning in one direction than it does in any other. Completing the days of your life in strict calendar order can feel forced. Arbitrary. Especially after you've seen what I've seen.

Most people I know live their lives moving in a constant forward direction, the whole time looking backward.

size of

Thirty-one is a smallish universe, slightly below average in size. On the cosmic scale, somewhere between shoe box and standard aquarium. Not big enough for space opera and anyway not zoned for it. Despite its relatively modest physical dimensions, inhabitants of 31 report a considerable variance in terms of psychological scale, probably owing to the significant inconsistency in conceptual density of the underlying fabric of this region of existence.

4

Universe 31 can feel claustrophobic some nights, like it's an overgrown city of insomniacs, crowded and noisy and suffused with a background illumination that glows purple in the sky, in the east sky and the west sky and in the north and the south, in the early sky and the late, high and low and in every corner of every sky, and on nights like these, no one ever sleeps in this city-sized universe, everyone just stares up at their vast yet tiny piece of the connected sky, listening to the still-humming hum of the primordial radiation.

Other nights, it's the opposite. It's so dark that every single person in the universe feels lonely, at the same time, even if they are holding someone or being held, and no one sleeps, because it's too quiet, too dissipated, everyone just lies awake feeling puny, feeling the enormity of what there is and what there isn't, everyone just stares upward at the heavens, watching their little corner, their swath of the frigid black cloth that swallows all warmth and light.

The usable interior volume of the main compartment of the TM-31 is a bit bigger than that of a phone booth. There isn't much extra room in here; in fact it's hardly a room at all, closer to a snug envelope of space–time that fits me like a second body. When I am looking through the viewfinder and I have the Frame of Reference filter set just right, I can, if I choose to, relax my mind in such a way as to imagine that I have actually become one with the device, have merged with it, and after a while the distinction between my vehicle and me gets a bit confused.

I guess I could describe this space as closest in size to, though not quite as large as, a hotel shower, not the kind with a curtain, but the cross-sectionally-square-shaped kind that is see-through from floor to ceiling, except that the main hatch to the TM-31, while it can be made transparent like a shower door (if that's what you're into), also happens to be a super-cooled magnetic compression system, designed to insulate against temperatures ranging from, at the low end, about half a degree above absolute zero to, at the high end, about a million degrees Kelvin. Hot, cold, people's opinions. All of it just bounces off. In addition, you can install an aftermarket cloaking device, so that the unit can be made invisible with the flick of a switch. You can just sit in here, impervious and invisible. So invisible you might even forget yourself.

Standing one way, with my arms outstretched, I can touch the sides of the unit with my palms flattened, but turning the other way, along the vehicle's lengthwise axis, I can't touch both sides with my full wingspan, and in fact, lying down in the unit along that axis, with my hair lightly brushing one wall, if I point my toes, I can just barely touch both ends with the entire height of my body. So that's how I sleep in here, i.e., quite comfortably. It's a bed, an office, a living room, and a tool shop. I take it to go to work, I use it for work, I go home from work in it, I live in it until the next day. If, in connection with a repair job, I have to do some back-of-the-envelope physics, nothing fancy, just some rough-and-ready number crunching, there's a space–time simulation engine with a touchscreen interface that offers drop-down menus with easy-to-use partial differential equations; all I need to do is click on what kind of geometry the universe has in the local region (Euclid/Riemann/Lobachevsky) and I'm off to the races. I have everything I need to move through time in here, and nothing I don't.

I will say, though, that it's hard to stay in shape in a recreational time travel device. I eat a lot of ramen. There isn't enough room to do push-ups. Sometimes I pick up Ed and curl him a few times. He grumbles a bit but puts up with it.

Because I have been living nonchronologically for so long, this device, this space in here is, in a way, for me, the world, the whole entire world. No other material entity has undergone the particular set and sequence of relativistic accelerations, of stresses and strains, of Lorentz contractions and time dilations, that this machine has. There is nothing in existence as similar to me as this TM-31. As a physical object, it encodes the history of my worldline. My personal time, as opposed to the external time of the world, exists inside here, and here only. The air in here, the molecules in here. My calculator, the shirt I'm wearing, my pillow, my quantum screwdriver, my Planck-length measuring tape. These are the objects that come with me as I move, as I tell the machine to move. The unit, this phone booth, this four-dimensional person-sized laboratory, I live in it, but, over time, through diffusion and breathing and particle exchange, the air in here, the air that travels with me, it is me, and I'm it.* The exhaled carbon dioxide that gets recycled and processed by the pump, the oxygen-rich air that is piped back in, these molecules* move around me, and in me, and then back out, all* of it* the same matter.* I breathe it* in, it* is in my bloodstream. Sometimes, they* are part of me, sometimes, I am part of them.* Sometimes, they* are in my sandwich,* sometimes in my hair,* sometimes in my blood*–brain* barrier,* sometimes in my foot,* sometimes even in my lungs* and stomach* and kidneys* and gallbladder,* sometimes in the on-board quantum* computer,* sometimes in my graph paper,* sometimes in the blood* coursing through my beating heart.* The photon,* the light* in here,* has been bouncing around for a while. It's* old light,* it's* new light,* it's* all* the same age, it's* all* the same light.*

*In Feynman's path integral formulation, a particle, any particle, a photon, say, is not so much a particular object at a particular location in space and time as it is an aggregate, a total, a sum over histories.

Put another way: a photon takes every possible path through space–time to get from point A to point B. In a sense, every photon in the universe is everywhere in the universe at every time in the universe.

Or, put yet another way: there is only one photon in the entire universe, and that photon, spread across all of creation in a vast probabilistic smear, that one photon is responsible for all the light we see.

reality, in relation to

Reality represents 13 percent of the total surface area and 17 percent of the total volume of Minor Universe 31. The remainder consists of a standard composite base SF substrate.

In terms of topology, the reality portions of 31 are concentrated in an inner core, with science fiction wrapped around it.

While it was long thought that reality was simply a special case of SF (i.e., QoE factor = 1, i.e., the strangeness of experience is no greater or less than intuitive notions of how things should be), it is now believed that, in some geological sense, the SF layer is structurally supported by the non-SF core of "reality," and researchers have recently begun to conduct experiments to study what they suspect may be an invisible, microscopic, but highly dynamic exchange of materials at the thin permeable boundary layer between the two regions.

5

When you are a kid, playing with the other kids on your street, and everyone is fighting over who they are going to be, you have to call dibs early, as soon as you see one another, pretty much as soon as you step outside your house, even if you're halfway down the block. First dibs gets Han Solo. Everyone knows that. You almost don't even have to say it. If you are first, you are Han Solo, period, end of story.

There was one time Donny, the kid from two blocks over (the other side of the freeway), got first pick and said he was going to be Buck Rogers, and everyone laughed at Donny so hard and for so long that he looked like he was going to cry. He begged to change his answer, but by then it was too late. Justin, who had second dibs, got to be Solo that day, which was like winning the lottery with a ticket he didn't even buy, and he milked it for all it was worth. Donny was in agony, was in hell really, and everyone called him Suck Rogers until he peed his pants and then got on his blue Huffy bike and rode away, never to return.

I was never totally sure why everyone wanted to be Han Solo. Maybe it was because he wasn't born into it, like Luke, with the birthright and the natural talent for the Force and the premade story. Solo had to make his own story. He was a freelance protagonist, a relatively ordinary guy who got to the major leagues by being quick with a gun and a joke. He was, basically, a hero because he was funny.

Whatever the reason, first place was always Solo, always, always, always, and second place was usually Chewbacca, because if you weren't the one saving the galaxy, you might as well be eight feet tall and covered with hair.

But no one grows up wanting to be the time machine repair guy.

No one says, Hey, I want to be the guy who fixes stuff.

My cousin is in accounts receivable on the Death Star, and whenever we talk he always says how nice it'd be if I joined him. He says they have a good cafeteria. So that's an option. And there's an opening for a caseworker at the social services bureau for noninteresting aliens. Government pension.

But really, it's probably just easiest to keep doing what I'm doing. You know how it goes. At first it's just for the time being, until you can get your own story together, be the hero in something of your own. You tell people it's your day job, you tell yourself it's your day job, and then, at some point, without you noticing, it stops being your day job and just becomes your job.

At least I get a gun. It's standard-issue to us service techs, for the rare occasion when a client refuses to cooperate and endangers himself or the structural integrity of the fabric of space–time. It's actually a pretty cool, semi-scary-looking gun, not at all wimpy. I've never used it, of course, but once in a while I'll take it out of the holster and pose with it in front of the mirror, just to see what I would look like arresting someone.

attachment coefficient

Inhabitants of Universe 31 are separated into two categories, protagonists and back office.

Protagonists may choose from any available genre. Currently, there are openings in steampunk.

Back office support workers must choose between retcon, accounting, human resources, time machine repair, or janitorial.

In order to qualify as a protagonist, a human must be able to demonstrate an attachment coefficient of at least 0.75. A coefficient of 1.00 or above is required in order to be a hero.

Factors used in calculating the coefficient include

- ability to believe
- fervency of that belief
- humility
- willingness to look stupid
- willingness to have heart broken

- willingness to see U31 as nonboring or, better yet, to see it as interesting, and maybe even important, and despite its deeply defective nature possibly even worth saving

Any inhabitant with a negative attachment coefficient (in which case it is referred to as a *coefficient of ironic detachment*) will be placed on probation pending review of the individual's suitability for continued inclusion within the U31 diegetic space.

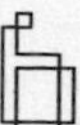

Chronodiegetics is the branch of science fictional science focusing on the physical and metaphysical properties of time given a finite and bounded diegesis. It is currently the best theory of the nature and function of time within a narrative space.

A man, as the theory goes, falling through time at a constant rate of acceleration, will not, absent any visual or other contextual clues, be able to distinguish between (i) acceleration caused by a force that is diegetical in nature and (ii) an extra-diegetical force. Which is to say, from the point of view of this man being pulled into the past, it is impossible to know if he is at rest in a narrated frame pulled by gravitational memory, or in an accelerated frame of narrative reference. The man experiences what is termed *past tense/memory equivalence*. In other words, a character within a story, or even a narrator, has, in general, no way of knowing whether or not he is in the past tense narration of a story, or is instead in the present tense (or some other tensed state of affairs) and merely reflecting upon the past. This equivalence forms the theoretical basis for an entire field, summarized as follows:

The Foundational Theory of Chronodiegetics

Within a science fictional space, memory and regret are, when taken together, the set of necessary and sufficient elements required to produce a time machine.

I.e., it is possible, in principle, to construct a universal time machine from no other components than (i) a piece of paper that is moved in two directions through a recording element, backward and forward, which (ii) performs only two basic operations, narration and the straightforward application of the past tense.

I remember there were Sunday afternoons in our house when it felt as if the only sound in the world was the ticking of the clock in our kitchen.

Our house was a collection of silences, each room a mute, empty frame, each of us three oscillating bodies (Mom, Dad, me) moving around in our own curved functions, from space to space, not making any noise, just waiting, waiting to wait, trying, for some reason, not to disrupt the field of silence, not to perturb the delicate equilibrium of the system. We wandered from room to room, just missing one another, on paths neither chosen by us nor random, but determined by our own particular characteristics, our own properties, unable to deviate, to break from our orbital loops, unable to do something as simple as walking into the next room where our beloved, our father, our mother, our child, our wife, our husband, was sitting, silent, waiting but not realizing it, waiting for someone to say something, anything, wanting to do it, yearning to do it, physically unable to bring ourselves to change our velocities.

My father sometimes said that his life was two-thirds disappointment. This was when he was in a good mood.

I guess it was a kind of self-deprecation. I always hoped but was afraid to ask if I had anything to do with the remaining one-third.

He had always been considered, by his colleagues and advisers and superiors, to be a very good scientist. I watched him through five-year-old eyes, and then through ten- and fifteen- and seventeen-year-old eyes, looked at him through a scrim of slight awe and fear.

"The only free man," he would say, "is one who doesn't work for anyone else." In later years, that became his thing, expounding on the tragedy of modern science fictional man: the desk job. The workweek was a structure, a grid, a matrix that held him in place, a path through time, the shortest distance between birth and death.

I noticed, on most nights, his jaw clenched at dinner, the way he closed his eyes slowly when my mother asked him about work, watched him stifle his own ambition, seeming to physically shrink with each professional defeat, watched him choke it down, with each year finding new and deep places to hide it all within himself, observed his absorption of tiny, daily frustrations that, over time (that one true damage-causing substance), accumulated into a reservoir of subterranean failure, like oil shale, like a volatile substance trapped in rock, a vast quantity of potential energy locked in to an inert substrate, unmoving and silent at the present moment but in actuality building pressure and growing more combustive with each passing year.

"It's not fair," my mom would say, setting his dinner on the table, trying to console him with a hand on his back. He'd flinch from her touch or, worse, pretend she wasn't there. We would all sit and eat in silence, and then my mother would go to her separate bedroom to read herself to sleep.

He kept index cards, three inches by five, in a metal box. They started as a kind of engineer's Rolodex: sparse, efficient, joyless. On each card, on the top red line, was a person's name, a friend or an acquaintance or a colleague, in his tight, clear, unerring hybrid of print and script. Underneath it, in the blue lines of the rest of the card, was written a phone number, and an address if he had one, and over to the right, some note on his relationship to, or the noteworthiness of, the person.

Harold Chen *Fluid Dynamics*

314-192-6535

—says he admires my thesis

—his son is looking for internship

Frank Lee *Damage and Durability*

271-828-1859

—possible project together?

—waiting to hear back

As a kid, I saw those cards as the beginning of something. I saw their ordered state, their formality, each one representing a connection to some outside mind, to other scientists. I saw that metal box as a treasure chest.

Looking back now, I realize how few cards there were, how carefully each one was written, I understand that this level of care was due to how sparse the contacts were, that the amount of time spent on each card was inversely proportional to the amount of connection my father actually had to the outside world.

I remember him sitting by the phone, his small, compact frame tense with anticipation, waiting there for a call that would be a big deal to him, a slight courtesy for the caller.

"I think the phone rang when you were out earlier," I would say sometimes.

"You didn't get it?"

"Just missed it."

"No message on the machine."

"I'm sure they'll call back."

The books in his study, with their rigid cloth spines and their impenetrable titles, they seemed daunting and impossible back then, but now, thinking back, I can see how the books were all related, I can see how they were, collectively, a bibliography of a career in striving, in aiming, in seeking to understand the world. My father searched for systems of thought, for patterns, rules, even instructions. Fake religions, real religions. How-to books. *Turn Three Thousand into Half a Million.* Turn half a million into ten. *Conquer Your Weaknesses.* Conquer yourself. *Inventory of Your Soul.* Take an inventory of your own failings. Higher mathematics and properties of materials, somber, gray monographs on single, esoteric subjects were side by side with books with bright red titles, titles dripping with superlatives, with promises of actualization, realization, books that diagrammed the self as a fixable lemon, self as a challenge in mechanics, self as an exercise in bullet points, self as a collection of traits to be altered, self as a DIY project. Self as a kind of problem to be solved.

When waiting by the phone got to be too much, he used to go to his room, change his clothes, and head down to the garage. I would wait a few minutes and head down there, stand near him, watch him tinker. If he couldn't figure something out, he'd go to the hardware store, leaving me there to dribble a mostly flat basketball until he came back. Sometimes he didn't come back for hours. When he did fix something, he would explain it to me, step by step. He was never happier than when he could walk me through a problem, from beginning to end, knowing at each juncture what the next step would be. I asked questions until I couldn't think of any more, and when we'd exhausted the subject, we'd head back upstairs, wash up, sink ourselves into the couch in front of the TV.

"What are we watching?" I would ask.

"Not sure. I think it's news from another world."

We'd watch in happy, tired silence. Mom would bring cut cubes of watermelon, pierced with toothpicks, and the three of us would press them into our mouths, drinking the cold juice.

"How is school?" my dad would say.

"Good, I guess."

"Tell me about it."

I would tell him about it, then we'd fall back into silence. After a while, he would lean back, close his eyes, smile.

"What do you think . . ."

A long pause.

"Dad?"

My mom would raise the back of her hand to her cheek. *Sleeping,* she would mouth at me.

Then all of a sudden: "Son." He'd snorted himself awake.

"You were saying something."

"Was I?" He would laugh a little. "I guess I'm a little sleepy."

"Can I ask you a question?"

"Sure."

This is what I should have asked him: If you ever got lost, and I had to find you, where would you be? Where should I go to find you?

I should have asked him that, a lot of things, everything. I should have asked him while I had a chance. But I never did. By then, he had drifted back to sleep again, smiling. Dreaming, too, I hoped.

My manager IMs me.

We get along pretty well. His name is Phil. Phil is an old copy of Microsoft Middle Manager 3.0. His passive-aggressive is set to low. Whoever configured him did me a solid.

The only thing, and this isn't really that big a deal, is that Phil thinks he's a real person. He likes to talk sports, and tease me about the cute girl in Dispatch, whom I always have to remind him I've never met, never even seen.

Phil's hologram head appears on my lap. I sort of cradle it in my hands.

YO DOG. JUST CHECKING IN.

HEY PHIL. EVERYTHING A-OK HERE. YOU?

YOU KNOW, SAME OLD. MY LADY IS STILL ON MY CASE ABOUT THE DRINKING. BUT YOU KNOW HOW I ROLL.

Phil has two imaginary kids with his wife. She's a spreadsheet program and she is a nice lady. Or lady program. She e-mails every year to remind me about his fake birthday. She knows they're both software, but she's never told him. I don't have the heart to tell him, either.

SO WHAT'S UP, PHIL?

OH RIGHT. WE CAN'T GUY-TALK ALL DAY, HA HA? I'M PUNCHING YOU IN THE ARM NOW, EMOTICON-WISE. I DON'T KNOW HOW TO CONVEY THAT. ANYWAY, MY RECORDS ARE SHOWING YOUR UNIT IS DUE FOR MAINTENANCE. YOU FEEL ME, DOG?

SHE'S RUNNING FINE.

TAMMY hears this and starts to make a noise like, uh, no she's not. I hit her mute button. She gives me a look.

YEAH, I KNOW, HOMIE, I KNOW.

SO WE'RE GOOD? WE'RE GOOD, RIGHT, PHIL?

Come on, Phil. I stroke his holographic hair. Come on, be a pal. Say it, Phil. Say we're good.

YO DOG YOU KNOW I'M YOUR BOY BUT, HEY, UH, YOU'VE BEEN OUT THERE AWHILE NOW, DOG, AND I DON'T KNOW, MAN, YOU KNOW?

Of course not. I monkey around with the Tense Operator for ten years and right when it starts breaking down is when I have to bring it in. I'm going to need to figure out how to fix it if I want to keep my job.

ALL RIGHT, DON'T SWEAT IT, PHIL. I'LL BRING IT IN. ANYTHING ELSE?

YO DOG, THAT'S TIGHT. WE'RE COOL, RIGHT? I'M STILL YOUR HOMIE? MAYBE WE CAN GRAB A BEER WHEN YOU'RE IN THE CITY. IS THAT RIGHT? GRAB A BEER? GRAB. GRAB. GRAB. GRAB. GRAB.

Phil crashes a lot, midsentence. Sooner or later, they're going to upgrade, and then no more Phil, and yeah it's true I could do without all the small talk, but I'm pretty sure I'll miss him.

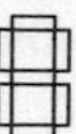

Client call. I punch in the coordinates and now I'm in the kitchen of an apartment, in Oakland, in Chinatown, sometime in the third quarter of the twentieth century. A pot of oxtail stew burbles on the stovetop, fills the room with a deep, rich cloud of stewiness, fills the room like a fog bank rolling over the bay.

I go into the living room and find a woman, a little younger than I am, maybe twenty-five, twenty-six. She's kneeling over a much older woman who lies still, in an awkward position, legs slumped off the couch, left arm dangling down to the floor, mouth slightly open as if she has lost control of it, eyes looking up at the ceiling, or whatever's beyond the ceiling, filled with a clear-eyed awareness of what's happening.

"She can't see you," I say to the younger woman.

"But I can see her," she says. She doesn't look up at me.

"Not really. This didn't really happen. You weren't there when she died."

Now the younger woman looks at me. Angry.

"Your mom?" I say.

"Grandmother," she says, and I realize in my time away from time, spent idling in my machine, I've become terrible at guessing someone's age.

I nod. We both watch the old woman lying there, coming to terms with whatever she was coming to terms with.

TAMMY discreetly beeps to remind me we have a job to do, rifts in the underlying fabric to repair. If we stay too long, the damage could get worse.

"I'm not saying this to hurt you," I say. "All I'm saying is that since you weren't there when this actually happened, you can't be here now."

She ignores me and doesn't take her eyes off her grandmother and for a while, I'm not sure she's heard or maybe she heard me but doesn't understand, but then she looks at me.

"So what is this? An illusion? A dream?"

"More like a window," I say, and I see that she gets it. "By using your time machine this way, you are creating a small porthole into another universe, a neighboring universe. One almost exactly like ours, except that in this alternate world you *were* there when she died. This living room, right now, is the vertex between Universe Thirty-one and Thirty-one-A, and you are bending space and time and light to see into the past, a false past, a past you wish you could go to. Although you can see, through this porthole, what happened back then over there, you're not really standing next to her. You are in your own universe, our universe. You are infinitely far away."

She takes a moment to digest this. I open up a side panel and immediately see the problem.

"You tampered with your tau modulator."

She gives me a guilty look.

"Don't worry," I say. "I see it all the time."

She looks back at the scene in front of us. "I was a sophomore in college. She was the only reason I even made it there," she says. "She called and I could hear something in her voice. I should have known. I should have known to come home."

"You had your own life to start."

"I could have come home. My dad told me it would be soon. I could have come home."

Grandma closes her eyes. A look of something unresolved twists across her face, and then a flicker of what could be disappointment, and then, exhausted, she takes her last breath, alone, the pot of stew untouched in the next room.

I wait for what I hope is a respectful interval of silence, then quietly finish the repair and go back into the kitchen to allow her a few more minutes. I can hear crying, then low talking, then what sounds like a song, once sung to a little girl maybe, now sung one final time. The stew smells really good. I'm trying to figure out if it will cause a paradox if I have a bowl when the young woman comes into the kitchen.

"Thanks for that," she says.

"Yeah, take all the time you want. Well, not all the time."

"I suppose I can't stay here."

I shake my head. "If you bend too much and for too long, the porthole becomes an actual hole, and you might end up over there."

"Maybe that's what I want."

"Trust me. It's not. That's not home. I know it seems like home, everything looks the same, but it's not. You weren't there. It will never be the case that you were."

A typical customer gets into a machine that can *literally* take her whenever she'd like to go. Do you want to know what the first stop usually is? Take a guess. Don't guess. You already know: the unhappiest day of her life.

Other people are just looking for weird. They want to turn their lives into something unrecognizable. I see a lot of men end up as their own uncles. Super-easy to avoid, totally dumb move. See it all the time. No need to go into details, but it obviously involves a time machine and you know what with you know who. General rule is you want to avoid having sex with anyone unless you are sure they aren't family. One guy I know ended up as his own sister.

But mostly, people aren't like that. They don't want trouble, they just don't know what else to do. I see a lot of regular offenders. People who can't stop trying to hurt themselves. People who can't stop doing stupid things because of their stupid hearts.

My vocational training was in the basics of closed time-like curves, but what they should have taught me was how that relates to people's regrets and mistakes, the loves of their lives that they let get away.

I've prevented suicides. I've watched people fall apart, marriages break up in slow motion, over and over and over again.

I have seen pretty much everything that can go wrong, the various and mysterious problems in contemporary time travel. You work in this business long enough and you know what you really do for a living. This is self-consciousness. I work in the self-consciousness industry.

nostalgia, underlying cosmological explanation for

Weak but detectable interaction between two neighboring universes that are otherwise not causally connected.

Manifests itself in humans as a feeling of missing a place one has never been, a place very much like one's home universe, or as a longing for versions of one's self that one will never, and can never know.

9

Sometimes I think back to when my father and I were first starting to sketch it out in his study at home, just ideas on a pad, just lines and vectors and tentative inequalities, first starting to realize what might be possible, and I suspect that he knew even then that he would get lost. It was almost like he was trying to get lost, like he knew what it would all lead to, this machine. He wanted to use it for sadness, to investigate the source of his own, his father's, and on and on, to the ultimate origin, some dark radiating body, trapped in its own severe curvature, cut off from the rest of the universe.

I remember the graph paper we used, the pattern of one-centimeter squares in a light green grid. My father would open a package of five pads, each one a hundred sheets thick. He used to open the package with his company-logo letter opener, pulling the letter opener out of its holder in the heavy brass piece sitting on top of his desk (I can still picture the black box it came in, with fancy gold cursive lettering on it—EXECUTIVE DESK SET—how at first, the words seemed like a kind of promise, a looking toward the future, a rare admission of his hope and ambition, and I can also picture the dust that gathered on the box, how, with each passing year that layer of dust thickened into a visible accumulation of embarrassment, how I wished I could have snuck into his office when he was at work and thrown that box away, or hidden it from him, so that word wouldn't have to be right there on this desk, staring him in the face every day, EXECUTIVE, a thoughtless word, a thoughtless gift from the company for ten years of unappreciated service).

He would worry the cellophane in a spot just a bit, just enough to pinch between his fingers a bit of the clear wrap and tear the membrane, making that delicate, fine-structured sound of it being torn.

"Ahhh," he would say, half smiling, enjoying the sound. He would hand me the wadded-up ball of cellophane, so I could crunch it in my hands and listen to it crackle back a bit, then crunch it harder and toss it into the gray wire wastebasket, where it would sit atop a sliding sheaf of bills and return envelopes for bills and credit card offers, an unstable mountain of debt and credit, an avalanche waiting to happen.

"Choose a world, any world," he liked to say. It was a stack of planes, an *n*-dimensional space–time, ready to be filled. I would take out one of the five pads and then he would put the rest back into his cabinet. The squares of the grid went all the way to the top, and the bottom, and the edges on either side, which was pleasing and Platonic and right. If there had been any sort of margin on the sides, or at the top, or any other kind of break in the Cartesian plane, something would have been lost, the ability of that graph paper to represent the total, the universal, the conceptual space would have been destroyed.

Where the pad was bound at the top there was a red, waxy strip, and sometimes my father would tear off the top sheet, so we could work on it without leaving impressions from our pen on the two or three or four (depending on how hard we pressed our pencil or pen) sheets below, and that sound would be somewhat similar but in many ways quite different from the ripping-cellophane sound, this one heavier, coarser, deeper, but more often my father wouldn't rip off a sheet at all, and instead leave the paper on the pad.

"Look at that," he said. "How the ink bleeds." He loved the way it looked, to write on a thick pillow of the pad, the way the thicker width of paper underneath was softer and allowed for a more cushiony interface between pen and surface, which meant more time the two would be in contact for any given point, allowing the fiber of the paper to pull, through capillary action, more ink from the pen, more ink, which meant more evenness of ink, a thicker, more even line, a line with character, with solidity. The pad, all those ninety-nine sheets underneath him, the hundred, the even number, ten to the second power, the exponent, the clean block of planes, the space–time, really, represented by that pad, all of the possible drawings, graphs, curves, relationships, all of the answers, questions, mysteries, all of the problems solvable in that space, in those sheets, in those squares.

"Today we will journey into Minkowski space," and with a few casual sweeps of his hand across the known world, what had been empty world was now a place full of direction and distance and invisible forces.

"Consider a body," he said, while drawing vectors and truths, "maybe a boy separated from his twin, and moving at the speed of light. Or a lonely astronaut, missing home."

I loved the way he used the paper, the whole paper, as a space, when he would write notes in the corner, or label the axes, or create a symbol key in the lower left-hand corner, or, best of all, draw a curve on the *x–y* plane and then write the equation for the curve $f(x)$ equals one-half *x* cubed plus four *x* squared plus nine *x* plus five, up in the upper left-hand corner of the graph, floating there in quadrant II of the Cartesian plane, that equation existing in science, in science fiction, in the realm of science fictional equations. I loved seeing his lettering, so neat, practiced from thousands upon thousands of hours of problem sets no doubt, both in school and after school and in his spare time and in his work and in his after-work brainstorming, and now with me, his son, his student, his would-be research assistant. Lettering so uniform, letters so straight and consistent in size and well lined they looked like words in comic book dialogue bubbles. I loved how my father set down the letters, mindful of the spacing, not fitting one to each box, which would have looked too structured, too planned, too spread out, not aesthetically pleasing, those letters would have looked like prisoners, each in solitary confinement, but rather, using the horizontal lines as a guideline, the words, the letters, crossing through and over and on top of the lines, no explanation, no protective underlining or boxing or any other kind of markings indicating a setting-off or a differentiation between text and curve, between space and commentary on the space. The words were right in there, close to the curve, close to the *y*-axis, just floating in the plane along with the graph, this space the Platonic realm, where curves and equations and axes and ideas coexisted, ontological equals, a democracy of conceptual inhabitants, no one class privileged over any other, no mixing or subdividing of abstractions and concrete objects, no mixing whatsoever. The words an actual part of it, the whole space inside the borders, the whole space useful and usable and possible, the whole, unbroken space a place where anything could be written, anything could be thought, or solved, or puzzled over, anything could be connected, plotted, analyzed, fixed, converted, where anything could be equalized, divided, isolated, understood.

My personal clock shows that I've been in here, more or less, for almost ten years. Nine years, nine months, and twenty-nine days, according to the subdermal biochronometric chip inserted just under the skin on my left wrist. That's how much time has passed for me, for my body, in my head. A rough measure of how many breaths I have taken, how many times I've closed and opened my eyes, how many lunches I have had in here, how many memories I have formed.

I guess that makes me thirty. Thirty-one-ish.

Probably goes without saying, but time machine repair guys don't get a lot of action. Had a one-night stand with something cute a couple of years ago. Not human exactly. Humanish. Close enough that she looked awesome with her shirt off. We hung out a few times, tried messing around but in the end I couldn't quite figure out her anatomy, or perhaps it was the other way around. There were some awkward moments. I think she had a good time anyway. I did. She was a good kisser. I just hope that was her mouth. Or at least her mouth-analogue.

In the end, it wasn't going to work. I don't think she had the brain chemistry for love. Or maybe that was me.

I don't even get much sexbot these days.

When you are thirteen, you spend all your time imagining what it would be like to live in a world where you could pay a robot for sex. And that sex would cost a dollar. And the only obstacle to getting sex would be making sure you had four quarters.

Then you grow up and it turns out you do live in that kind of world. A world with coin-operated sexbots. And it's not really as great as you thought it would be. Partly because it doesn't make you any less lonely in the perpetual dark of total vacuum and partly because, well, it's gross. Your friends, your neighbors, your own family, they know what you are doing in the kiosk. They know because they do it themselves. Partly because sexbot technology hasn't really improved much since the first-generation consoles. No one cares enough. For a dollar, it's pretty hard to complain.

Living like this means the year stops making sense, and the month and the week. The dates fall away from the days, like glass punched out of window frames, or ice cubes out of a tray into a sink, identical, dateless, nameless durational blobs, melting into an undifferentiated puddle. Is that a Saturday, a Friday, a Monday? Is that an April 13, or a November 2? Living like this means you don't have a container anymore for the different days, can't hold in a little twenty-four-hour-sized box a set of events that constitute a unit, something you can compartmentalize, something with a beginning and an end, something to fill with a to-do list. Living like this means that it all runs together, a cold and bright December morning with your father or a lazy evening in late August, one of those sunsets that seem to take longer than is possible, where the sun just refuses to go down, where the hour seems to elongate to the point that it doesn't seem like it can stretch any farther without detaching completely from the hour before it, like a piece of taffy, like undersea molten lava forming a new island, a piece of time detaching from the seafloor and floating up to the surface.

It's not comfortable in here. But it's not *not* comfortable, either. It's neutral, it's the null point on the comfort–discomfort axis, the exact fulcrum, the precise coordinate located between the half infinity of positive comfort values to the right and the half infinity of negative values on the left. To live in here is to live at the origin, at zero, neither present nor absent, a denial of self- and creature-hood to an arbitrarily small epsilon–delta limit.

Can you live your whole life at zero? Can you live your entire life in the exact point between comfort and discomfort? You can in this device. My father designed it that way. Don't ask me why. If I knew the answer to that, I would know a whole lot of other things, too. Things like why he left, where he is, what he's doing, when he's coming back, if he's coming back.

Where has he been all these years? I'm guessing that's where he is now.

I don't miss him anymore. Most of the time, anyway. I want to. I wish I could but unfortunately, it's true: time does heal. It will do so whether you like it or not, and there's nothing anyone can do about it. If you're not careful, time will take away everything that ever hurt you, everything you have ever lost, and replace it with knowledge. Time is a machine: it will convert your pain into experience. Raw data will be compiled, will be translated into a more comprehensible language. The individual events of your life will be transmuted into another substance called memory and in the mechanism something will be lost and you will never be able to reverse it, you will never again have the original moment back in its uncategorized, preprocessed state. It will force you to move on and you will not have a choice in the matter.

10

Phil was right. I was overdue for maintenance. The Tense Operator is pretty much kaput.

TAMMY doesn't think we have enough power to even get back to corporate HQ. Ed is licking his own stomach like crazy, like he's trying to hurt himself. Which is what he does when he's nervous. He gives me a look like, *You're the human. Do something.*

"Is it my fault?" TAMMY says. She always thinks everything is her fault.

"No, it's my fault."

"Is it my fault that it's your fault?"

"I don't even know what that means. I guess so. If that's what you want."

"Thanks," TAMMY says, and she seems pleased.

The truth is, I broke the Tense Operator by living in between tenses. I broke it through my cheating, wishy-washy way of moving through time. It used to be that you could cheat the machine by leaving it between gears, living in a kind of half-assed way, present and at the same time not quite in the present, hovering, floating, used to be you could avoid ever pinning yourself down to any particular moment, could go through life never actually being where you are. Or I suppose, more accurately, being *when* you are. That's what P-I allows, a convenience mode.

But I abused it. It's not supposed to be used as the primary driver of chronogrammatical transport. It isn't designed for that kind of use: the Present-Indefinite isn't even a real gear. It's like cruise control. It's a gadget, a gimmick, a temporary crutch, a holding place. It is hated by purists and engineers, equally. It's bad for aesthetics, bad for design, bad for fuel efficiency. It's bad for the machine. To run in P-I is to burn needless fuel in order to avoid straightforward travel. It's what allows me to live achronologically, to suppress memory, to ignore the future, to see everything as present. I've been a bad pilot, a bad passenger, a bad employee. A bad son.

Ed sighs. Dog sighs are some form of distilled truth. What does he know? What do dogs know? Ed sighs like he knows the truth about me and he loves me anyway.

I ask TAMMY what her optimism is set at. She says very low. I tell her to just move it up one notch, to normal low, and recalculate.

"What do the numbers say now?"

"We'll make it to HQ. But just barely. There is an eighty-nine percent chance the machine will be damaged in the crash."

I tell her she can do it. That I believe in her. I say it sincerely, because I do believe in her.

"You are good," I say.

"No I'm not. I'm not. I'm not. I'm not," she says. "I'm no good."

And then, softly, to herself: "Am I?"

. . .

True to her calculations, TAMMY gets us there.

Flying into the center of the universe, even a smallish universe like this one, is something you never get used to.

It's like flying into LaGuardia at sunrise, which is no coincidence, since a little over one-third of the greater metropolitan area of the capital city of Minor Universe 31 just happens to be made up of what used to be New York City.

As the machine banks into its approach and we angle into our steep descent spiral, looking down into the city, I have, for a minute or two, some clarified sense of scale, the proper balance of awe and possibility, a kind of airplane courage. Perspective. That's what I have, only it's not in space. It's perspective in time. Instead of gliding down over and then into the skyline, we glide down over, and then into, the present, and what always gets me is the quality of the light, the way it just starts to reach my eyes, to gather around me, gather itself up, to see what light looks like as we slow down from relativistic speed.

Sliding into the time corridor, you can see it all, the spiky skyline, high and low points in the overall texture and layout of the past and future of this place, the mix of styles and the clash of lines and planes. All of these people, all so small and compartmentalized. In space and time. You see the paths of moving objects: people in high-rises, people in their office buildings with the fake plants and the elevators going up and down and at their desks and moving around, an entire day's worth of movements, an entire day all at once, not a blur, not an average, but the totality of a day.

All these people with so much less control over their own velocities than they think they have.

All these people who go on like this, moving around in their patterns, and I am one of them, stuck in my own pattern, I am perhaps the worst of them, but for now, in this instant, I can see what I am.

Even the stationary objects, you see how they sway and torque, shear and bend, how they wear down slightly, erode even within the course of a day, they become averages of themselves over time.

As I'm landing I focus in particular on one man, a stranger, someone I can pick out maybe because he looks like me, about my height, my weight, my age, but unlike me he's wearing a suit, he looks like a family man, coming home from work. I can see this man at the end of his day, but at the same time I can see him waking up this morning, and I can see what happened to him in between, how he started with a hope of what today would bring, and how it didn't bring that, and how he doesn't know that yet, and how he already does. I can see him in the day, and see the day in him, see how he doesn't move through time so much as he is made of time, or at least his life is, and what that means, I can see it not as frames in a movie, not as the flicker of a flipbook, but the whole flipbook itself.

capital city

Eighty-seven percent of the nonrobot population of Universe 31 lives in the capital city, the full legal name of which (used only by nonlocals due to the fact that it is printed that way on maps) is, officially,

NEW ANGELES/LOST TOKYO-2

The name is abbreviated in governmental regulatory usage as NA/LT-2, and is sometimes, though not frequently, referred to informally as Lost City or Verse City or New Tokyo, but is known to virtually everyone other than tourists and bureaucrats as Loop City.

The formation of Loop City occurred in two steps. Step one: the cities of New York and Los Angeles, 2,462 miles apart, much to the surprise and consternation of residents and property owners and municipal officials and parking lot owners and westsiders from the eastern half and eastsiders from the western half, slowly and invisibly and irreversibly merged into each other, in the process swallowing up what was in between, leaving one metropolis that contained, within it, what had been America. Alaska and Hawaii were included as well.

The second phase began a short while later, when the sprawling city of Greater Tokyo spontaneously bifurcated along a spatio-temporal fault line. Half of this bifurcated Tokyo moved across the world and wrapped itself around the perimeter of the recently formed New York/Los Angeles chimera. This half is referred to as Lost Tokyo-2.

The other half, Lost Tokyo-1, has not been located yet, although presumably it exists out there somewhere in the universe, a mega-demi-city of eighty-five million people, a city fractured, cracked in half, torn, ripped not cleanly, but shredded, ragged, ripped along living rooms, plans, meetings, dates, conjugal beds in prisons, family dinner tables, secrets being whispered into ears, couples holding hands, separated in an instant without warning or explanation, leaving two halves, bewildered, speaking Japanese to instant neighbors from the other side of the world, unable to understand what has happened, or if things will ever go back to the way they were, hoping its other half might someday find its way back.

11

The hub is jammed, so subspace traffic control pushes us out into a holding pattern, where we end up spending almost two hours of bio-time in the XPO loop. By the time I get clearance to an open channel, I'm hungry and tired and then they tell me the first available channel for my reentry into time is a few minutes before midnight. Which, at first, I'm thinking, *That's just great, what that really means is that my choices for food are the all-night corner deli or the gritty little two-bucks-for-two-hot-dogs place on 72nd and Broadway,* but then I'm thinking, *Eh, who am I kidding, I like those hot dogs.*

After landing, we taxi from our time capture cage over to the maintenance facility. Ed and I climb out of our TM-31 and into the cavernous space of Hangar 157.

The repair bot—they program these bots with Simulated Mechanic Guy personality—takes one look at my TM-31 and raises his eyebrows at me.

"What is that?" I say. "Don't do that."

"Do what?"

"You know what. With your eyebrows. What am I saying? Those aren't even real eyebrows."

"Someone's a little defensive."

It kills me to admit it, but he's right. I am defensive about my machine. You can tell a lot about a person by the wear pattern on his chronodiegetic manifold. It's really nothing but your anxieties and tendencies and thought patterns, etched in chromium dioxide.

He tells me to come back tomorrow. I say what time. He says before noon.

"Can you be a little more specific? I mean, you're a robot. You do have Microsoft Outlook Seventy-three-point-zero loaded into your brain."

"Fine," he says. He rolls his eyes in simulated contempt and beeps out a calculation.

"Eleven forty-seven. Your machine will be ready at eleven forty-seven on the dot tomorrow. Don't be late."

On the subway, the guy next to me has his head in a news cloud. *Paradox is up 16 percent.* If I lean in a couple of inches, I can just make out what it says. *Up 16 percent in the fourth quarter on a year-over-year basis.* If everyone would just stop trying to kill their grandfathers, maybe we could get things under control. We may not be able to change the past, but nevertheless, we still manage to screw things up fairly well.

The guy reaches his stop and gets off, leaving his news cloud behind. I love watching the way these clouds break up, little wisps of information trailing off like a flickering tail, a dragon's tail of typewriter keys and wind chimes, those little monochrome green cloudlets, a fog of fragments and images and words. On busy news days, the entire city is awash in these cloudlets, like fifty million newspapers brought to breathing, blaring life, and then obliterated into a sea of disintegrating light and noise.

Coming up the stairs out of the station and into the center of the city, the center of the universe, you can be forgiven for feeling, if just for a moment, that you are walking into a place where the ordinary laws of science fiction do not apply.

You stand and walk and wait and move on a series of shifting colored neon platforms, each one drenched in a different trademarked color scheme, wrapped in all directions with a protected corporate logo.

You're a character at the beginning of a fully rendered, immersive environment video game, the world laid out before you, a series of challenges, an endless scrolling realm full of periodically oscillating dangers.

Tonight, I feel small. An entire night in the city seems to be too much for me, too immense for me to not get lost in. By now it's past one, the after-hours city is in full swing, and morning is a long way off. Between now and sunrise, anything could happen. And there it is, the feeling comes back, like a coldness in my legs, a tingling up the back of my skull and down my arms. I had forgotten: this is what it feels like to live in time. The lurching forward, the sensation of falling off a cliff into darkness, and then landing abruptly, surprised, confused, and then starting the whole process again in the next moment, doing that over and over again, falling into each instant of time and then climbing back up only to repeat the process. I almost missed this buzzing, gauzy field of vision, the periscoped consciousness, the friction and traction of being in my own life, of using it up, had almost forgotten the danger and pleasure of living in the present, the chaotic, slapdash, yet overproduced stage-scene of each moment, assembling itself then disbanding, each moment taking itself apart, just like that, the sets struck, each instant in time falling apart just as it is coming together.

I stand there for a while, shivering, stuck, trapped, free, until I look down and notice that Ed looks a little cold. I get a hot chocolate from a guy with a cart, and two hot dogs, one with ketchup and one without, and Ed and I split everything, although if we're being honest, I think he probably eats a little more than his share.

Ed wants to see the meson-boson show, so we cross the street and stand outside for a while, watching a replay of the Big Bang. At the top of the hour, they open a box and every color in the universe comes pouring out, refracted and reflected, bouncing around inside the window display. Ed lets out a few sharp yaps of excitement, and a few people slow down to watch, but most have seen it before.

We cross the street to the opposite corner where an old man and some kind of genius baby play eleven-dimensional music on a four-handed instrument. The air above our heads is a smoggy miasma: mostly a vaporous fog of news and lies, mixed in with gaseous-form gossip, meme-puffs, and as always, the mists of undirected prayers. Men on corners whisper about secret shows upstairs.

I toss some change in the genius baby's hat and we continue through the square, trying to avoid all the bots, selling memories, selling. The digital Doomsday Clock says the world will end on schedule next week. The Dirac Foundation has purchased its own billboard, a calculator, twenty stories high, showing the Cumulative Aggregate Error in the universe. Ed and I watch the number get bigger for a while.

When Ed's seen enough, we walk back uptown, toward the building where I rent a room. Not an apartment. Just a room. An icy little box for me and my things, a place for a mattress and a toothbrush and a small couch and an almost useless television. I don't keep anything of importance in here. It just wouldn't make sense to do anything more permanent in the real-time world. I'm not here enough.

I get the key from the guy at the front counter. From his stationary, non-time-traveling perspective, he sees me almost every day, only each time he sees me, I've aged a year or two or five or nine. I rented the room when I got the job, ten biological years ago for me. To him, it was last Wednesday. My whole life will probably amount to about a month's rent, by his calculations.

I find a scratchy wool blanket in the closet, shake it out, and lay it on the couch for Ed. I go down the hall to the community sink to fill a dish of water, and even though he doesn't actually need it because he has no actual physical body anymore, Ed's appreciative. If I could be half the person my dog is, I would be twice the human I am.

corporate ownership of

After its initial owner gave up any serious ambitions for Minor Universe 31, the property was placed into turnaround, where it languished for a while before being picked up by a new operator.

Eventually, Time Warner Time, a division of Google, acquired the rights to 31 and completed the build-out, with visions of a middle-market to upper-middle-market asset and revenue stream, a branded corporate experiential shopping center, and the main attraction, a sparkling new four-dimensional theme park, complete with monorail and gift shop.

During the interim period, certain operators, especially those running major universes, used 31 as an unofficial storage space for their slightly damaged inventory, including experimental species, space stations, single-purpose planets that have been deserted or near deserted, and even entire genre system production facilities.

Other operators used 31 for the still somewhat controversial but increasingly common practice known as hypothetical mining, also known as weird farming.

The conditions of a place like 31, with its incomplete conceptual framework, regions of exposed wireframe structure, lack of complexity in terms of story line geometries, and dearth of heroes, provides an ideal environment for corporate operators to test out new ideas, allowing them to proliferate without worry of what will happen to the generally expendable, low-self-esteem human population within the space.

12

Once upon a time, I am ten years old and my dad is driving me home from the park.

We're floating through the streets in our family car, a rust-red Ford LTD station wagon with the windows covered in a layer of dust and the loose suspension that makes it feel less like a car and more like a scrappy little boat sailing down the avenue. I am tired and sweat-crusted and eating half of an orange Popsicle.

Sitting here in the front next to my dad, he in his uncomfortable-looking blue-gray slacks that he always wears, even on Saturdays, me in soccer shorts, sun beating down on my head, so hot even my hair is hot, my legs stuck to the vinyl seat, trying to concentrate on not letting the melting rivulets of orange-flavored sugar water run too far down the side of my skinny forearm, squinting through the windshield. I remember this day, I know what happens, and yet I still feel like I don't know what will happen.

"Kids at school say that you," I start to say.

"That I? I'm what?"

"That you're, uh."

"Strange?"

"Crazy."

I actually say this. I remember saying this. I remember regretting that I had said it even as I was saying it. I regret it even now. Regret what it started, regret all that came after.

He keeps his eyes on the road. I can't tell if he's mad. He doesn't say anything. I'm scared I've angered him somehow; I have a ten-year-old's crude sense of having found a subject that is dangerous, a son's sense of having wandered into the line of fire, into some sort of yet-to-be-discovered axis running between my father and me, and yet, and still, for some reason I keep going. Not to hurt him, no, I keep going just because, for the first time in my young life, it feels like my father is here, in the car, with me, listening to me, that for the first time ever I have his attention not as a boy, his son, but as a person, as a future man, as someone who is just starting to go out into the world and bring parts of it back, parts that can remind him that I won't always be his to teach, parts that may remind him of how small our family is.

I ask him if it's true what they say.

He says what's that.

"Do you really think it's possible to travel to the past?"

He's got to be mad now. He doesn't get mad often, but when he does. Not good. I'm sure he's mad, I'm positive, I'm considering how much it would hurt if I opened the car door and just jumped out, but then he just laughs and takes his foot off the gas and pulls into the slow lane. "We're time traveling right now," he says, the cars speeding by and honking in Dopplerized frequencies.

And then he pulls completely off the road into the parking lot of a video rental store and shuts off the engine and I am thinking he's doing this to somehow prove his point even further, that he's going to explain to me how even now, completely motionless, we are still time traveling, I am thinking I'm about to get a lecture about how I would understand this if I just kept up with my math homework, but instead, my father turns to me and tells me, in all seriousness, this idea he has had, a secret plan, an *invention.*

My father, the inventor. I had never thought of him that way before that afternoon, although a small part of me felt lifted, opened, as if the world was bigger than I'd imagined, that there were parts of my father I could never have guessed at. I thought of him as old, as someone with a job, as, well, Dad. Not someone with dreams or ideas. My father had ambition. Ambition he had never previously shared with me, and why would he, I was ten, but he also didn't share it with my mother, or anyone else. He kept it inside, in his study, in a box, in himself.

My father had originally come from a faraway country, a part of reality, a tiny island in the ocean, a different part of the planet, really, a different time, where people still farmed with water buffalo and believed that stories, like life, were all straight lines of chronology, where there was enough magic left in the real, in the humidity of August and the mosquito and the sun and birth, enough magic and terror in the strangeness of family itself, that time travel devices were not only unnecessary, but would have diminished the world, would have changed its mechanic, its web of invisible dynamics. The technology of the day was enough, the technology of the sunrise and sunset, the week of work and rest in cycles, in rhythm, sixteen hours of hard rice-farming labor, the remainder of time in a day left for eating and sleeping, the seasons, the years passing by, each one a perfect machine.

As he described his invention to me, I found it hard to look at him. He was talking a little too loud, for one thing, which, if you knew my father, was alarming all by itself. My father was quiet, but not meek, soft-spoken but not unsure. It was more than that. Quiet speaking was more than just a controlled softness of the voice, more than the virtues of decorum and tact and propriety. Quiet speaking was more than manners, or a personal preference or style, or personality in total. It was a way of moving about the world, my father's way of moving through the world. It was a survival strategy for a recent immigrant to a new continent of opportunity, a land of possibility, to the science fictional area where he had come, on scholarship, with nothing to his name but a small green suitcase, a lamp that his aunt gave him, and fifty dollars, which became forty-seven after exchanging currency at the airport.

And here he was, voice raw, talking fast, excited in a way that made me uncomfortable, hopeful in a way that worried me. I didn't believe it, or maybe I didn't believe in him, maybe I'd absorbed enough defeat in my short life from watching him, the look on his face as he pulled into the driveway every night, that I already doubted my own father. I thought he was brilliant, of course, he was my father, and a hero, but would the world understand him? Would the world give him what he deserved? There were opposing vectors, stress from the tensors pulling between what was and what could be, between his science fictional hopes and the reality of the station wagon we were sitting in.

He spilled out his secret theory in an excited rush, and part of me was thrilled that he wanted to tell me this, that I mattered to him, that I was grown-up enough to trust with his idea, with his hope, with his plan, but I couldn't show any of that to him, so I just stared straight ahead, through our grit-coated windshield, at the posters in the window for *Back to the Future* and *Peggy Sue Got Married* and *Terminator*. All of those stories about time travel, they were comforting, and at the same time it bothered me how they always made it seem fun and how everything fit into place, how things could only ever be how they were supposed to be, how the heroes found a way to change the world while still obeying the laws of physics.

I remember my mind drifting to the last time our family had gone into the video store, together, how my mom and dad took forever picking a movie and I'd wandered off and found, next to the licorice and cardboard boxes of chocolate-covered raisins, a comic book. The story itself was a trifle, some sort of third-class superhero, a forgettable guy with some useless power. It was something else in the book that caught my attention.

Way in the back of the comic, in the advertisement pages, in the lower left-hand quadrant of the second to last page, a little box, there was a rectangular ad, maybe four inches by five, that read at the top, in bold all-caps:

CHRONO-
ADVENTURER
SURVIVAL KIT

There were no exclamation points or any squiggly lines indicating weirdness or jokiness, or any other graphics to signify, This is for kids, this is a toy, this is just make-believe. It just had those words, and it was dead serious. Finding that little box of text, with those words in there, felt like I'd found a secret, a technology no one else knew about, something that might help me be the hero of the block, that might help my dad be the hero at his work, that might even help my dad and mom.

For five dollars and ninety-five cents, plus a self-addressed stamped nine-by-twelve envelope, sent to a PO box somewhere in a faraway state, the good people at Future Enterprises Inc. would send you a survival kit "of great use and convenience for any traveler who finds himself stranded on an alien world."

Half of me knew it was stupid. I was old enough to know better, but on the other hand, that font! Those letters in all-caps. It didn't look attractive and well formatted, the kind of thing a kid's eye would be drawn to; it looked like it came from a typewriter, unevenly spaced, like there was too much text, too many ideas and words and things that someone had to say, had to let people know about, it looked like it came from the mind of a brilliant, lonely, forty-year-old man, sitting somewhere in his basement in that faraway state, half crazy, sure, but *on to something*.

According to the ad, the kit had over seventeen pieces, but from the picture I could only see a plastic knife and a Chrono-Adventurer patch to sew on your clothes, and a map of the terrain of the science fictional universe, and what looked like a decoder, which I figured was for translating languages spoken by different life-forms—all of which totaled four pieces. I wondered what the other thirteen pieces were.

The ad said the kit was your only chance for survival in the harsh environment of an alien universe, but what I remember the most was the picture in the ad, not even a picture, but a tiny line drawing of a boy and his father, holding hands, not smiling, just staring out at you from their little box in the text, buried in the corner of the back page of that comic, and the ad didn't say, but it was reasonable to assume, to a ten-year-old me, that they were unlucky enough to have been stranded, but at least they had gotten the kit.

This is what I was thinking about when my father, a little out of breath, finished telling me everything he had kept bottled up inside, when he had finally confessed his most guarded dreams and stopped talking. For a long moment, it was silent in the car, and then he turned to me.

"So," my father said, "what do you think?"

I shrugged and kept my eyes fixed on the families in the window of the video store choosing their movies together, ready for a night of fun and popcorn.

"Dad," I said, "are we poor?"

I remember he was just starting to look disappointed that I wasn't at least a little bit excited. Then I said it. To this day, I don't know why I said it, where it came from. I was ten years old, he was my father, I wouldn't want to hurt him, couldn't know cruelty yet, what or why or how to be cruel. Could I? Did I? Of course I did. Maybe I'd learned it from the kids at school, had already incorporated it into my own growing theory of the world. Maybe I'd absorbed the capacity to hurt someone by listening to my parents every night, who were under the impression that turning the volume on the television all the way up somehow drowned out the voices, when the truth was and is (and my father, of all people, should have known this about the physical properties of materials, about what goes through walls, what moves through houses, what is muffled and what makes it through): everything gets transmitted. Call it the law of conservation of parental anger. It may change forms, may appear to dissipate, but draw a big box around the whole space, and add up everything inside the box, and when you've accounted for everything you find that it's all there, in one phase or another, bouncing around, some of it reflected, some of it absorbed by the smaller bodies in the house. The edge in their voices and turning up the TV only meant that I listened to them destroy each other to a sound track of *Fantasy Island* or *The Incredible Hulk* or *The Love Boat*.

Even now, to this day, I don't know if I said it because I was thinking about that survival kit, which I knew I couldn't ask him for, although I wasn't sure why, exactly, not this month, maybe for Christmas, or maybe next year. I didn't know why exactly, I just knew not to do it without anyone having to tell me, and that made me sad for my father, but at the same time it made me a little mad.

Maybe I just wanted a reaction from the man, who was so often cold and distant with Mom and even sometimes with me, the same man who had just now spoken to me about math and science and science fiction with more passion than I had ever seen him speak about anything. I wanted a reaction and I was sure I'd gotten it. He had to be mad now, I thought, but I was wrong again. He just started the car and backed out without a word.

I spent the rest of the drive home with a puddle of melted Popsicle juice pooling on the top of my tightly clenched fist, afraid to move, surprised that he didn't even look a little mad. He just looked embarrassed. Or really, he looked crushed.

And in truth, I was half asking and half not-really-asking-but-knowing-the-answer, and I think that mixture of genuinely not understanding and half starting to understand the reality of our family, of my father and his job and his dreams and our car and our neighborhood, it did something to him. It hurt him deeply, but maybe also lit a fire in him, it put a distance between us that would persist for years into the future, and yet it opened up something between us, a channel, an axis, a direct line for honest communication.

socioeconomic strata

Minor Universe 31 is composed of three basic regions, which are sometimes informally referred to as *neighborhoods*.

At the lower end of the scale are the unincorporated areas, which have, as the name suggests, no particular look and feel, no genre.

Although sometimes referred to as "reality," it should be stressed that this layer of Universe 31 is quantitatively, but not qualitatively, different from the other regions. The difference is one of degree, not nature.

On the other end of the scale, the affluent inhabitants of the upper-middle to upper-end neighborhoods, perhaps searching for authenticity, or nostalgic for a different age, devote significant amounts of their time and resources to the creation of a simulated version of the unincorporated areas. Considerable expense is required for the upkeep of these highly stylized "reality" gardens, with the verisimilitude of one's personal family garden being a point of pride and a symbol of status among this stratum of inhabitants.

The remainder of the SF jurisdiction is occupied by the large, stable, middle-class regions, i.e., the subdivided science fictional zones, which make up the bulk of Universe 31.

A few decades ago, it became permissible for families to emigrate from the unincorporated areas of "reality" into the science fictional zones.

Permissibility, however, has not necessarily translated into economic permeability.

Despite improvement in recent years, successful transition into the SF zone remains difficult to achieve for many immigrant families, and even after decades of an earnest and often desperate striving for acceptance and assimilation, many remain in the lower-middle reaches of the zone, along the border between SF and "reality."

Although technically SF, the look and feel of the world in these borderline neighborhoods is less thoroughly executed than elsewhere in the region, and outcomes of story lines can be more randomized, due to a comparatively weaker buffer from the effects of 31's incomplete physics. As a result, the overall quality of experience for the residents of these striving areas is thinner, poorer, and less substantial than of those in the middle and upper regions, while at the same time, due to its mixed and random and unthemed nature, less satisfying than that of reality, which, although gritty, is, at least, internally consistent.

13

You can get into a lot of trouble in the city when you live like I do.

I've been on the job for a decade of my life now, but it's only been a week since I was last in the city. All the techs talk about how weird it is. You forget that your life is a short window, that you are stuck in the present, forget how your life is still here, waiting for you, wondering where you are, going on without you. You forget that people know who you are, think about you, might even be happy to see you.

I don't feel like running into anyone now, though. I'm only here for a night, and I have nothing to show for my lost decade except for biweekly paychecks from the company that, year after year, broke my father's heart.

I take the subway uptown, to the second-to-last stop. I find my way through the old neighborhood, around the all-concrete park where it's a bad idea to walk this late, up the little hill near where the subway comes above ground, turn the corner and there it is.

From where I'm standing near the dumpsters, I can see my mom in the window of the kitchen. It's two thirty-one and fifty-eight seconds in the morning. At two thirty-two she will look up, smile. She looks up, smiles. She's washing vegetables.

She's on the second floor. I jump and catch the ladder, pull myself up onto the fire escape, get a footing on the outside rail, and jump over. She's got her back to me. I duck down, watch her moving around the kitchen, setting the table for two.

"Come in," she says. "You want me to squeeze you some orange juice?"

She's not talking to me, of course. Well, me, but not me. She's in the prepaid time loop, living the same stretch of her life, over and over again. It's only an hour, which is what she can afford. I told her I'd help her upgrade, maybe ninety minutes, but she just patted my hand and said she would let me take care of her when I made it big. Whatever that means.

She goes over to the counter, heaps food onto a plate, and sets it down in front of my chair. She looks up, like she's remembering something, almost as if she could sense me here.

"Hi, Mom," someone behind me says, and she turns to look out the window. It's my hologram me, coming up the fire escape, the way I just did.

"Get inside," she says. "It's cold."

"Love you," hologram me says.

"Scoop the rice."

I watch my ghost-self eat as she continues to move around the kitchen, the whole time, never really looking at hologram me, just as she never really looked at me, either. She just wants someone to take care of, something to worry about. That's all. That's enough. I'm watching her idea of me, who is, in turn, watching her. She's just going about her business.

After a while, my ears and nose are cold enough that it occurs to me that I should check my watch. Twenty-eight minutes, right on time.

She clears all the plates, washes them, and starts cooking again. I recognize this part. The loop is about to end. Before it can reset, I tap on the window, lightly so as not to scare her, but she nearly falls down in fright anyway.

She snaps out of her time loop, groggy. Not quite happy to see me. It's been so long that it almost hurts her more that I'm here. This brief visit is just a reminder of how long it will be until the next one.

She opens the window, doesn't invite me in.

"You never call. You should call more often."

"I know, I know."

"I don't like it in here. Why did you stick me in here? Can you please take me out? I don't like it in here."

"I didn't stick you in there, Ma."

"I know, I know. You're a good boy."

"No I'm not."

"Okay, you're not."

"I'm sorry, Ma."

"It's okay."

"You don't want to know what I'm sorry for?"

"You never call."

"That's not it."

"Then what are you sorry for?"

"Forget it, Ma. I don't know. Forget it."

"You're a good boy."

"I better get going, Ma."

"I know, I know. You have a life. It's okay."

"I'll call more often. I will."

"No you won't," she says. "Wait here." She turns and walks out of the kitchen.

I learned grammar from my mom, who knew it well, considering she was not a native speaker, hadn't even learned English until she immigrated here. She, like my father, had come from that little island in reality, where they spoke their language, a home language, a private, family language, as well as the mainland language taught in schools by the nationalists, and so this language that I speak, the only one I know how to speak, was actually her third language, and a distant third at that.

And yet she speaks it well, well enough, considering all that, even if she is always translating in her head, even if she never became fluent like my father, never quite able to think fluently in English, and who could blame her? The tenses are so complicated, had never quite made sense to her, as they didn't work the same way in her language, one based largely on the infinitive.

When my mother taught me grammar, me at the kitchen table with a worksheet and blanks to fill in and verbs to conjugate, she was doing the dishes, cooking dinner, mopping the floor, I was six years old, I was seven, eight years old, I was young, I was hers, still her mama's boy, I hadn't yet entered the father–son axis, the continuum of expectation and competition and striving, I hadn't yet left the comfortable and snug envelope of the mother-space, I hadn't gone outside these parameters, out into the larger, free-form world of science fiction. My first understanding of grammar came from her, which is to say, my first understanding of chronogrammatical principles, of the present, the past, the future. I fall/I fell/I will fall. I am a good boy. I will always be her boy. I don't know what I would do without you. I don't know what I will do without you. I learned about the future tense, how anxiety is encoded into our sentences, our conditionals, our thoughts, how worry is encoded into language itself, into grammar.

Worry was my mother's mechanic, her mechanism for engaging with the machinery of living. Worry was an anchor for her, a hook, something to clutch on to in the world. Worry was a box to live inside of, worry a mechanism for evading the present, for re-creating the past, for dealing with the future.

After a few minutes, my mother comes back into the kitchen holding a box. She brings it over and sets it on the windowsill between us.

"I found this yesterday, in your closet." It's roughly the size and dimensions of a shoe box, wrapped in brown parcel paper. There don't appear to be any seams or folds in the paper.

"Yesterday? Why were you out of the loop? Why were you going through my stuff?"

"You don't live here anymore. You have so many clothes you never wear."

"Ma, those are from, like, fifteen years ago."

"So? They're not good enough for you? You don't remember, you asked me to buy those clothes. I bought them for you. See, I'm wearing your sweatshirt now. See? Fits. You have so many comic books. They are probably worth a lot now. Can you sell them? You should sell them. I will find them for you and you can sell them. Such a waste."

"You didn't answer my question."

"What's that?"

"Have you been living outside the loop?"

"You think it's enough? You got me a pretty nice one, okay, but you thought that would do it, that would take care of me, for the rest of, for good?"

"Mom. God, Ma. You just say that to me, like that, this late? Now? Why didn't you, God, why didn't you say something earlier?"

"Early when? Tonight? Last year? When you were first showing me the brochure?"

"Jesus, Ma. I'm, I'm sorry."

"You can't stay. I know. I know. Can you stay? I know you can't. Can you? Just a little while?"

"Ma."

"I know, I know."

"You know I want to, Ma. I can't. You know I can't."

"Okay, okay, bye. No sorry. You are a good son. No sorry, okay? I have to cook now. It's okay."

She shuts the window, turns, and goes back into her sixty-minute life.

On the way home, I see a lonely sexbot standing next to an empty glass vending case. She's an older model, on the plump side of zaftig, a face so sweet it's wrong to look anywhere but at her eyes, but I do anyway. Dark-haired with a hairstyle that seems slightly out of date, but then again, of all people, I'm not really one to talk.

I try to walk past, but she flags me down. Something about the look in her eyes gets me, even though I know they aren't really eyes.

She asks if I could loan her a little bit.

I say what for.

She says nobody buys her anymore, so she wants to buy herself.

I fish a bill out of my pocket. It's a five.

"This probably won't get you much time with yourself."

"Actually," she says, "that's a lot," and she looks so happy about the five-dollar bill that it makes me feel sad. Even the sexbots here are lonely. There really aren't even any bad guys anymore. I'm not sure there ever were. Everyone's always questioning themselves. Am I doing this right, is this how I'm supposed to look? Am I good enough to be a good guy, am I bad enough to be a bad guy?

Up the street a song cloud floats by, sagging a bit, but still intact. I walk faster and catch up with it just in time to hear the ending, a symphony orchestra, the sound full and resplendent, and it is one of those times, you know those times every so often when you hear the right piece of music at the right time, and it just makes you think, *This music didn't come from here, it was given, it fell from some other universe,* and it reminds you of that other universe, some place you've never seen but in your mind you know is there, because you have felt it, this special universe, stranger and better than the ordinary one, and you hang on to the sound of the violins for as long as you can, savoring the feeling of that special universe and wondering if you'll ever get to go there and also wondering if maybe we don't realize it, but we're in that one already, and we have been all along.

By the time I get back to my room, it's almost five in the morning. Ed, a bit confused, still gets up to greet me.

I take my toothbrush and a facecloth down to the sink at the end of the hall. Who is that, in the mirror? That's me, in the past, a moment ago, when the light bounced off me. I brush and spit, wipe my face hard to get the grime of the city off me. A lot of news and vapors and sexbot perfume are floating around in the atmosphere here. After a night out in the lost half city, you end up with the dust of dead robots in your hair, or someone's dreams, or their nightmares.

As I'm falling asleep, I can see, out the window, the fracture line of the disintegrated city, where this minor universe was left undone, not quite finished. Maybe it's just something I imagine in the last moment before sleep, but I swear what I see, behind a peeled-back corner of the sky, is another layer underneath us, a second, hidden layer, one that is present at every point, and always has been.

convenience, particular sadness of

Services available in the city include

- Ex-Girlfriend Hologram
- Pay-per-minute Alternate History Viewing Booth

Products available in the city include

- False Memories of Home (chewing gum)
- Aerosol Essence of Nostalgia for Summers Past
- Nearly six thousand varieties of sexbots
- Drinking buddy bots
- Friendbots, of varying humanness

14

When it happens, this is what happens: I shoot myself.

Not, you know, my self self. My future self. I shoot my future self.

What was I supposed to do? What else could I have done?

After my night out walking in the cold city, my body, unaccustomed to the exertion, had crashed, and when I woke up to the late-morning sun in my face, I knew something was wrong. I'd way overslept and woken up a quarter past eleven, thrown everything into my bag, grabbed Ed with one arm and the parcel my mom had given me in the other arm, and hustled down to Hangar 157, which is where I am now.

The clock says eleven forty-five as I run into this vast, climate-controlled space. Two minutes to go. I put Ed down and we run together, down endless aisles of identical-looking TM-31 machines, turning right and then left and right up until we get to the designated space, cage number 31-31-A, with, by my watch, eleven seconds to spare.

And there's that jerk of a repair bot, watching the gigantic overhead floating clock display, counting down the seconds, hoping I'll be late, and as I'm running up to my machine, I see a guy, future me, stepping out of that machine, with his own Ed the dog, future Ed, and his own service tool backpack, and even carrying his own brown-paper-wrapped parcel, and I guess I panic, because everything they ever tell you about what to do when you see yourself in a science fictional universe just goes out the window, and I take my corporate-issue prototype paradox neutralization concept weapon, and I point it at his chest and he reaches out with his right hand and he tries to pull the barrel of the gun down and what happens is that instead of the chest, I end up shooting him, once, in the stomach, just as he is saying something to me, it all happens very quickly but what I am pretty sure he says is

"It's all in the book. The book is the key."

and I don't know yet what the hell that means or even what book he's talking about but in any event it's too late because I've already squeezed the trigger, activating the facility-wide alarm system, and there are klaxons and flashing lights and some kind of whooping noise and an official-sounding voice comes on the PA system, saying something official-sounding, and the two-mile-square hangar gets turned into one deafening echo chamber, and the future Ed flips out and runs away, because shit, I just killed my own future, and I think for an instant about chasing after Ed but I see corporate cops running up the aisles at me from all four directions, so I have no choice but to jump into the time machine that future me was coming out of, my time machine, which I suppose is his, too, but I notice a little too late that the hatch is only part of the way open and so I bang my knee against the silver-iridium alloy edge of the TM-31's hatch, I bang it about as hard as I can imagine banging it without it actually shattering into tiny knee-shards, and I do an awkward and terrible half-somersault tumble into my machine, headfirst, while screaming in pain at TAMMY to go go go go go go go.

PARTIAL MAP OF CY'S TIME LOOP

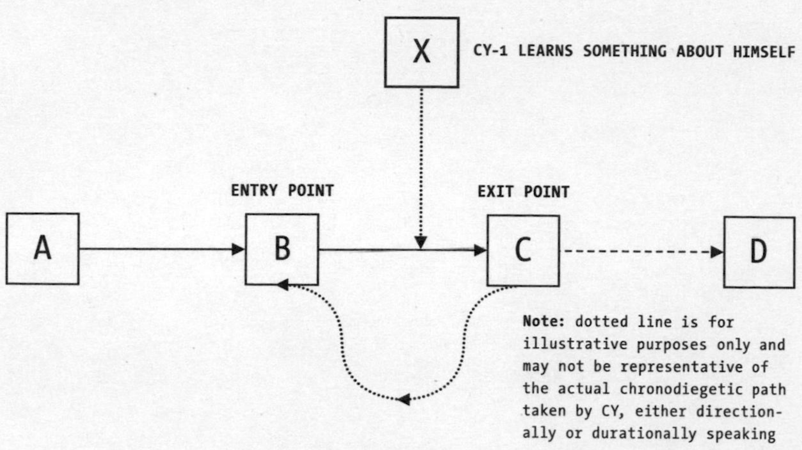
X
CY-1 LEARNS SOMETHING ABOUT HIMSELF
ENTRY POINT
EXIT POINT
A
B
C
D
Note: dotted line is for illustrative purposes only and may not be representative of the actual chronodiegetic path taken by CY, either directionally or durationally speaking

KEY:

CY-1 = "present" Charles Yu
CY-2 = "future" Charles Yu
A = CY-1 drops off TM-31 at Hangar 157
B = CY-1 sees CY-2 exiting TM-31, shoots CY-2
C = CY-1 travels in TM-31 back to event B, knowing that upon exiting the machine, he will be in the position of CY-2, and will be shot by himself, CY-1
D = some mysterious future event that CY-1 cannot get to
X = some point in time when CY-1 learns something important about himself
▲BC = the interval between events B and C represents the "length" of the loop

NOTES:

- The volumetric integral of the function defined by the loop represents the maximum amount of life that CY-1 can have, including joy and pain.
- A looped life is conventionally defined as one in which the time traveler necessarily suspends his own memory in order to continue on.
- The actual length of ▲BC may be significantly different from the subjective psychological duration experienced by a past-oriented traveler within the loop, e.g., it might feel like a month, but only be a moment.

(module β)

in the event you find yourself trapped in a time loop

(i) See if you can figure out the sequence of events that make up the loop.

(ii) The thing to remember is this: the fact that you are in a time loop is most likely your fault.

(iii) You are the one who interacted with yourself, for whatever reason you thought you had.

(iv) Assuming you want to stay in your current universe, you will need to be able to reproduce your actions exactly in order to avoid inadvertently changing your own past and thereby diverting yourself into a different, alternate universe.

(v) Once you have established the sequence of events, see if you can figure out why these things are happening.

(vi) Try to determine what, if anything, you can learn about yourself from this time loop.

(vii) In most cases, you will not learn anything. You will just go around and around, until you get bored enough that you decide to escape, even if it means losing your own life, exiting the universe for another one.

15

Back in my time machine. My leg is throbbing. I am trying to pull up my pant leg to inspect the damage.

Damn it all to hell.

This is not good.

It's the day everyone dreads. Your life stops moving forward and starts going in a circle.

I'm in a time loop.

TAMMY tells me not to beat myself up. She says it happens to everyone, some even by choice. I say my mom doesn't count. Moms don't count. I say, Yeah, but usually it happens to action heroes, to people with stories to tell. It doesn't happen to people so young, who've done so little with life, usually it doesn't happen in such a dumb way. I shot my own future. In the stomach.

I've gotten myself into a time loop and I guess I can stop caring now, realizing that my path is set.

On top of all of that, as I'm pulling out of the hangar, I see Ed down there, looking up at me, tongue hanging out, confused.

. . .

Phil calls.

He doesn't IM, he actually calls, uses his simulated human speech syllabic conversion mimicry feature to talk to me, but being Phil, he doesn't know that's what it is. He just thinks it's his voice.

"Hape al, wha ta ha pend b-b-back there?" he says, sounding a little bit like a Speak and Spell, and a little bit like a five-year-old boy doing his impression of a robot.

"I don't know, man. I just freaked. I saw myself coming toward me and I thought no way I'm going to let this idiot trap me in a time loop."

"There is no ree zun to run. I said it! Did you hear that? That was a good sentence I said. You doan tuh have to run. Come ba-a-ack to huheadquarters."

"You know I can't do that, Phil."

"S-s-sure you can. Wee ull have a beer, we'll work ih tout."

"We can't, Phil. We can't have a beer. You know why?" And here it goes again. Ever catch yourself in the middle of saying something you know you'll regret? Something so mean you know you should stop immediately but some part of your brain kicks in and won't let you stop?

"You're a computer program, Phil. Didn't you know that? You never noticed that about yourself? Go ahead, I'll give you a second to check."

And then there's an awful silence while he checks. It's like that day in the car in front of the video store with my dad, that day all over again.

When he comes back, he's given up using the voice.

IT APPEARS YOU ARE CORRECT. I AM A MANAGER PROGRAM. I GUESS I SHOULD PROBABLY GO TELL MY WIFE.

JESUS. PHIL. I'M SORRY. I SHOULDN'T HAVE SAID THAT. I WAS KIDDING.

WAIT. OH. SHE'S NOT REAL, EITHER, IS SHE? I SUPPOSE I DON'T HAVE ANY KIDS, THEN?

PHIL, LISTEN. I'M SO SORRY. FORGET I SAID IT. LET'S GO BACK TO BEFORE I TOLD YOU THAT.

I CAN'T FORGET IT. I'M INCAPABLE. THAT MUST BE NICE, BEING ABLE TO FORGET. IS IT NICE?

The worst part is that Phil isn't even mad. He can't get mad, he doesn't have that feature.

WELL, I GUESS IT'S FOR THE BETTER THAT YOU TOLD ME THIS. THE TRUTH IS ALWAYS BETTER, I SUPPOSE. I SHOULD GET GOING. MAYBE WE'LL HAVE THAT BEER SOON. HA HA. JUST KIDDING. I KNOW THAT'S NOT POSSIBLE. YOU CAN HAVE A BEER AND I'LL JUST, UH, ADD SOME NUMBERS UP OR SOMETHING.

TAMMY makes the face for Slightly Disapproving, which is about as harsh as she knows how to be. "What the hell are you looking at?" I say, too mean, meaner than I mean to be, just way too mean.

. . .

TAMMY hibernates in order to cool off, leaving me alone, drifting in my own time-free silence. I guess in a way, this is what I want. To push everyone and everything away. I have this way of doing this. There are so few moments when the opportunity presents itself to really make a choice. So often, it's just the story line of the world propelling me forward, but there are these key nodes, branches in the timeline, when I can exercise some free will, and they always seem to turn out this way, always seem to end up with me hurting someone I love, someone I should be protecting. I'm nice to strangers who break their time machines, nice to random sexbots who ask for money, but when it comes to the people I care about the most, this is what I do. My mom, Phil, my dad.

I can blame this stupid defective universe where everyone is always so sad there aren't even any bad guys anymore, but what if there never were any bad guys? Just guys like me. I'm the bad guy. No heroes, either. I'm the hero. A guy who just shot his own future in the stomach.

Maybe that's what my future was trying to tell me. That it's not worth it. Maybe he was trying to end it all. Either he shoots me and creates a paradox, or I shoot him, and cut off my own future. Either way, problem solved, no more having to worry about anything. I wish I could take it back, go back to just before I ruined Phil's day, ruined his whole life, and let myself shoot me, since I'm the one who deserves it. But I guess all things in due time. At least I know I'm going to get what's coming to me.

I notice there's a book on my console. I pick it up, run my hand over the back cover. I've never seen it before, but it feels familiar already, a part of me already knows what this is. I turn the book over and read the title of this book, in my hands. It's called *How to Live Safely in a Science Fictional Universe*.

page 101

In the book, right at this point, my future self has written these words: *There exists a time in which you will have written this book.*

In the next paragraph, he goes on: *I know none of this seems very believable. It probably doesn't even make sense. But for once in your life, please, I am asking you to trust me. Trust yourself.*

16

It's a slim, silver-colored volume with a metallic-looking sheen, relatively modest in size but with a surprising heft, as if it acquired some amount of relativistic mass in its journeys around time. It has the kind of unexpected density that academic press books (even the paperbacks) often have, due in part to a thicker paper stock and in part to the weight of a more substantial ink, the sneaky heftiness of the book being the aggregate cumulative effect of hundreds of thousands of individually insubstantial little markings, letters and numbers, commas and periods and colons and dashes, each symbol pressed upon the page by the printing machine with a slightly greater-than-expected force and darkness and permanence.

Apparently, I'm going to write this book, which appears to be, as far as I can tell, part engineering field manual and part autobiography. Or rather, I already wrote it. Now I just have to write it, which is to say, I have to get to the point in time when I will have written it, and then travel back in time to get shot and then give it to myself, so I can write it. Which all makes sense to me, except for one thing: why the hell would I want to do any of that?

Normally, when someone says trust me, I find it hard to trust him anymore, and this is doubly true for when it is my self who is saying it, but as it turns out, in my science fictional studies, I once took a course on the topological properties of possibility space and in chapter three of the coursebook we had covered this very scenario as a case study in this:

Exceedingly Improbable yet Hypothetically Still Possible
States of Affairs in a Coherent Universe
Governed by a Consistent Set of Fictional Laws

and in fact, for a while I even considered writing my thesis on a minor but novel approach to proving, with only ZF+CH (Zermelo-Frankel set theory plus the Continuum Hypothesis), that this exact fact pattern, the one happening to me right that moment, was in fact (i) grammatically allowed, (ii) logically permitted, and (iii) metaphysically possible. And of course, my future self would know all of this, and he would know that I would know that he would know this, and that's why he knew it would be worth it to give me this book. And so he's written, in his handwriting, handwriting I recognize as my very own, these words:

Read this book. Then write it. Your life depends on it.

TAMMY says that I'm supposed to place the book within the TM-31's read/write device. She opens up a panel on my right side I've never actually seen before, and out from it comes a clear Lucite block.

"This is the TM-Thirty-one Textual Object Analysis Device," she says, or TOAD for short.

Who's in charge of acronyms on these things, I say.

The TOAD opens up on hinges, like a book itself, revealing a carved-out rectangular space. TAMMY tells me to put the book in there.

The hinged cover closes, and the TOAD retracts back into the side of the unit, so that it is flush, and all that's left visible is the silver cover, title, floating there.

"It has a reinforced titanium-unobtainium alloy nanofiber running through it, which allows it to record any changes you make to the text on a real-time basis."

And so I'm reading this book and somehow in act of reading it, I am, with the help of TOAD and TAMMY, creating a copy of it, in a very real sense I'm generating a new version, actually, that is being simultaneously written into and stored in TAMMY's memory banks. In doing this, I am making the book my own, in retyping a book that already exists in the future, producing the very book I will eventually write. I am transcribing a book that I have, in a sense, not yet written, and in another sense, have always written, and in another sense, am currently writing, and in another sense, am always writing, and in another sense, will never write.

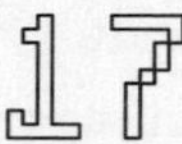

from How to Live Safely in a Science Fictional Universe

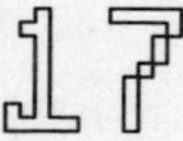

At the present moment, I am, in fact, reading the text display generated by TOAD on the main screen in front of me, going along through the words and, noticing, here and there, that the words seem to slightly adjust themselves, sometimes a little ahead of where I'm reading, but usually just behind what I've read, as if the device is self-editing, modifying the text to fit as closely as possible the actual throughput of my conscious act of reading it. In essence, my reading is a creative act, the product of which is being captured by the TOAD. I'm typing, even though strictly speaking I am using the TM-31's cognitive-visual-motor-sound-activated recording module, which operates, as you might guess, by simultaneously tracking output from the user's neural activity, voice, finger movements, retinal movements, and facial muscle contractions. It's part keyboard, part microphone, part optical scan, and part brain scan. When I want to type, I raise my hands up in front of me, palms down, in a position approximating typing, and a virtual QWERTY layout materializes in front of me. When I want to switch to voice, I just start reading the book, and the unit switches to an auditory-recognition transcription system, converting my voice into modifications in the written text. If I get tired of typing and voice modes, I can simply read the text to myself, and the unit will track my eye movements to determine, with near-perfect accuracy, what word I am reading, based on the minute ups and downs, lefts and rights of my retinas, and then matching those movements, using brain activity data as a kind of rough double check, against the blood flow and heat output of various areas of my language- and concept-processing lobes and sublobes of my brain.

I can switch back and forth among these three modes seamlessly, sometimes even using more than one at a time, and even using all three, so that the machine is tracking my voice, my eyes, my mind, and my finger movements all at once. In the typing-only mode, the unit tracks just my fingers. The same goes for the voice-only mode, i.e., even though I necessarily must use my eyes and brain to read the text in order to pronounce the words out loud, if I choose the voice-only mode, the device does not track my eye movements or brain activity, and only the microphone records the words I am speaking. There are advantages and disadvantages to each mode, and to the various combinations of modes.

Currently I am using both the reading and typing modes. This is because the copy of this book that my future self gave to me was apparently damaged at some point in time (perhaps, as TAMMY suggests, it was damaged in the very act of transferring it to me, a strange sort of loop indeed). As a result, some of the words are illegible. There are blurry areas where the paper has absorbed moisture, and portions that have faded due to the cumulative effects of light over time. There are other places where the text has been scratched out, in some instances by what appears to have been, based on the seemingly random pattern of mechanical injury to the book, some sort of accidental scraping or sharp impact, as if it had been slammed against an extremely hard and thin object, like perhaps the edge of a table (or a time machine door), and in other instances by what seems to have been very deliberate redaction by way of defacement, as if an X-Acto knife or other implement had been applied with precision and intent to excise particular words and sentences.

For instance, right here, the next paragraph begins with the words *what if,* and after those words there is a depression, where the fibers of the paper show evidence of having been pressed down and rubbed vigorously, and what remains is a gray smear of what may have been one or more additional words, as if someone, maybe a reader, maybe the previous owner of this copy, or maybe even me, at some point in the future, wanted to destroy or conceal or confuse the meaning of such a paragraph, so that the question that remains is only:

What if  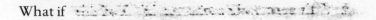

with no context or other indication of what the rest of the sentence was, or if there even was a rest of the sentence.

Perhaps even more disturbing than the fact that there are missing and damaged words and sentences in the text is that there are places where the book, this book, is simply blank (even though I am pretty sure this makes no sense, since how can I know there will be blanks when I have not, by my own admission, read ahead to see any blanks yet and there haven't been any so far, I'm still performing the read/write/self-edit process as faithfully as I can, in fact, even this parenthetical aside has been worded exactly as I am recording it, right up to the words I am typing right now and now and now and now, I am typing what appears to be somewhat digressive and extemporaneous rambling, all of which is starting to make me have serious doubts in terms of the whole free will versus determinism situation because even as I am typing from the copy I have in my hand, the text is matching my thoughts exactly, all the way down to—EUREKA!—that random word I just interjected there, or attempted to interject, that word, *Eureka,* having occurred in the text at the precise moment I had decided, internally, to inject a random word in an attempt to diverge from the text, and now, having failed in that attempt, realizing I had better stop now and end this sentence before I dig myself any deeper into metaphysical trouble).

There are gaps, blanks, throughout, which I will need to fill in. There are gaps in my autobiography.

Here is one such gap.*

* NB: This is how the text actually reads in the copy I am working from. The text also includes this explanatory (and somewhat self-referential) footnote, including this second sentence, which is itself a second-order meta-explanation of the already explanatory first sentence. It is unclear what the function of this self-referentiality is, other than to raise doubts in my mind as to the actual provenance of this manuscript, although I do note that this third sentence, just like the rest of this footnote, is also in the text I am copying from, verbatim, which makes it seem almost as if I am, in a way, telling myself what to think, that my future self has produced a record of the output of my consciousness, of my internal monologue. Or rather, a dialogue, between myself and my future self, in which my future self is telling my present self what I have already finished thinking but have not yet realized I thought.

This is consistent with Libet (1983).

And here is another gap.*

*Let's suppose that I, being a volitional agent, am presented with a choice: I can have either a cookie from Jar A or a cookie from Jar B. After evaluating both cookies, at some point in time I form the intention to take a cookie from Jar A, and then, at a later point in time, I actuate the movement of my arm toward Jar A in furtherance of my choice. This is, intuitively, one might even say obviously, the order in which events occur.

Except that it isn't.

After Libet, we now know that I actually began moving my arm toward Jar A *before I became aware of my own conscious decision to choose Jar A*. In effect, I decided to reach for the cookie in Jar A before I realized that I made the decision. The question is, which I was I? Which I am I? Am I the decider-I or the realizer-I? Both? Neither?

I am currently reproducing this as correctly as I can, interpolating where necessary, based on my best guess about what I wrote, or would have written, or will write. As a result, I'm not sure this is going to turn out to be exactly the same book as the one I was given, prior to it being damaged and redacted. I doubt it is, or will be, or could be. My job, though, isn't to figure it out or create it, because it has, to the extent it ever will be, already been created, and figured out. I don't know the ending because, as I mentioned, I am reading along as I type this. This is a document that came from nowhere. This is a chunk of information created spontaneously out of nothing, filtered through my interpretation and memory.

Just to be sure, I have run this set of propositions, the text so far, through TAMMY's onboard Plausibility Verification Unit, and it has confirmed that my future self was telling the truth. The book, its existence, its creation, is the product of a causal loop. It comes from nowhere, has no unique origin, and yet its creator is me.

"This book," TAMMY says to me, "is a copy of a copy of a copy, and so on, forever, like that, I could keep going if you'd like." It is a copy of something that doesn't exist yet. It is a book copied from itself.

Life is, to some extent, an extended dialogue with your future self about how exactly you are going to let yourself down over the coming years.

There is a sense in which I am the author of this book, and a sense in which I am merely its first reader. I am writing this book at the same time I read it, I am typing while reading it, while thinking it, switching at will among all three modes, both actively and passively receiving and creating it, this book that matches the moment-by-moment output of my consciousness, gaps and all, and even as I attempt to fill in these gaps, and interpret my own life story before I know what happens, I am learning about what my life will be, what it is now, what it already has been, I am seeing this book for the first time, word by word, reproducing it from sensory data with my eyes and fingers and brain and voice, while also seeing it from direct experience exactly as it is, while at the same time interpreting it, a story about my father and me and the various time machines, all of the machines we have been in together, a story given to me by my future self.

I am editing this book even as I write it, writing it as I read it, now I am repeating myself, even as I create it, I know it is flawed and possibly even inconsistent, and yet all I can do is to go forward and see where it takes me, all I can do is to go backward and see where it takes me, all I can do is read it to see what happens to my father, what happened to him, to us, to see if it is true, to learn what I am apparently thinking right now, to learn what I will think, to see if I can make any sense out of his life. Which is what sons do for their time-traveling fathers, act as biographers for them, as science fictional biographers, as literary executors, taking the inheritance of the contents of their fathers' lives, given to them in an unprocessed jumble, out of order and nonsensical. Sons do this for their fathers, they use their time machines and all of the technology inside, and they see if it is possible to put those contents into a story, into a life, into a life story. There is a sense in which I am pretty sure this makes no sense. I don't know where this is going. I don't know how it ends.

residual objects in closed time-like curves

In any coherent time loop, there are certain objects that are created during and exist within the time loop. One common example of such an item is the hypothetical Book from Nowhere: A man brings a copy of a book with him back in time, giving it to himself, and instructing himself to reproduce the book as faithfully as he can. The book is then published, and after its publication, the man then buys the book, gets in a time machine, and starts the cycle all over again. The book is a perfectly stable physical object that actually exists, despite the fact that it seems to come from nowhere.

Less certain is whether human memory works the same way.

18

"Why can't I just give up now?" I ask TAMMY.

"I don't think it works that way," she says, but I don't see why it shouldn't. Today should be the first day of the part of my life where I can stop caring. Right? I can just go around in this loop, because in the end, I'm going to end up where I know I'm going to end up anyway, and that's that. It literally does not matter anymore. Today is the beginning of the end. Or the end of the beginning. I killed my future, I am my future, I am going back to my past to do it all over again. A tidy loop.

"Wait a minute. Don't you go through the loop? Should you have some kind of record, some residual memory, some counter for each iteration? How many times have I done this? A hundred? A thousand? Do I ever learn anything from it? Do I ever become a better person?"

"My records show that this is the first time."

How many times have I even been through this loop? TAMMY says just once. She says this is the first time she has been on this path. This may be a time loop, but it's the first time through.

I say she's lying. She reminds me that she's incapable of lying to me, and I realize her answer makes sense. If the loop is exactly the same set of events every time, she wouldn't have any way of distinguishing them. To her, it's only one set of events that occur in a set period of time, and there's no marker, no higher-level counter, no internal-state reflector that records separate impressions. Her memory doesn't work that way, is what I realize, and then I realize something about what I just realized. My memory doesn't work that way, either. I have no way of knowing how long I've been in this loop, and I'll never know. I'm just going around and around on this thing, however long it is, an hour, a day, my entire life, each time as oblivious as the last time, each time as scared as if it's my first.

I am a passive observer in this, this record of my own time loop. But why? Why should I be passive? Why not go straight to it, straight to the thing I am driving at, the thing I am being driven toward, to the heart of it, the heart, his heart, the truth, the end, the only thing that matters? Why not go to the moment when this all ends and I say what I end up saying, and let that be what it is? Why bother with all of this outer shell, this casing, this surrounding bulk of matter, this envelope, this container, these words, this intervening buffer between now and the time I want to go to? What is stopping me? As far as I can tell, nothing. Nothing is stopping me from just jumping ahead to the end in my reading/writing/whatever-it-is-I-am-doing in "creating" this whatever-this-object-is. This book, this autobiography, this self-instruction manual (self-coercion manual, self-creation manual), this set of operating parameters for a time machine, this laboratory space for the design and performance of what appears, so far, to be an ill-advised and poorly conceived chronodiegetic experiment.

But what if I were to skip forward? Just cut out all of this filler in the middle. After all, as my self told me, I am the author of this. Whatever it is. I am its author and its only reader.

I want to know what happens. I want to know if I'll ever get out of here. I want to know if I'll ever see my father again. My mother again. I want to know if this is how my life will go, until it just ends.

TAMMY says: not a good idea.

TOAD says: not a good idea.

I punch in the instruction: go to the last page.

19

Not a good idea. Immediately after sending the instruction, I begin to feel a vibration, slight but detectable, of the walls of the TM-31.

I hit a button and the hatch decompresses. I pop open the door. This is what I see:

[this page intentionally left blank]

And now the TM-31 starts to vibrate, at first gently, then more vigorously, like an unbalanced centrifuge. Indicator lights are blinking.

TAMMY informs me, in a neutral but slightly concerned tone, that I have set the time machine on a noncomputable path.

What was I thinking? Because, if I'm being honest, I'm not sure I would even know what I do with myself. Even if you could skip to the end of it all, what would I do the next day with my life that would be so different from all the days that came before? What miraculous change would I make, after getting out of this rut, what new kind of person would I choose to be that next day? And the next? And how about the day after, and all of the days after that?

The TM-31 is shaking pretty good now. The tone of TAMMY's voice has modulated from mild concern to slight alarm. What have I done? Oh, crap, duh. It's Time Machine Circuitry 101. Overriding TOAD's analysis algorithm has tripped the causal wiring between TOAD and TAMMY, which is something I wish I'd thought of a few minutes ago.

(At this point, the vibration of the machine, up until now low and erratic, speeds up to what must be a resonant frequency, because the entire unit starts to rattle. The housing for the decoherence module comes loose and crashes to the floor, leaving the guts of the machine slightly exposed, the naked physicality of the thing, the purely material bits, the wiring and the diodes of the randomness generator left vulnerable to damage, to being overwhelmed with data, the data of the world, the datum that is the world, all the other data from all possible worlds, all the could-worlds and should-worlds and would-have-been-worlds, the kind of tiny hidden world only detectable with the ultra-high-sensitivity receptors set to the exact specifications necessary to perceive it.)

Then: nothing.

20

I wake up in an enormous Buddhist temple. I am standing in the vestibule of what appears to be the main hall. The air is cool and smells of incense. It is dark. The small amount of sunlight coming through the space underneath and between the doors feels like an intrusion into this rarefied place.

There are no clocks in here.

Two wooden railings separate the vestibule from the main room. Between the railings is an opening, and to either side, people have left their shoes. There are small blue slippers available, into which I slip my tube-socked feet. The insides of the slippers are cool on the tops of my toes and the outside edges of my feet.

Among all of the slippers, I see a pair of worn brown men's dress shoes, which look vaguely familiar.

I'm standing just at the edge of the large rectangle that makes up the main space of the room, at the end of what feels like two square miles of deep burgundy carpet. Three Buddha statues sit at the far end of the room, raised up on platforms, looking over my head, out toward infinity. Not looking, I suppose, but seeing.

On the left and on the right are doors into side rooms, each one dedicated to a subsidiary higher being, specialized Buddhas: the Buddha of Familial Relations, the Buddha of Safe Passage, the Buddha of Everlasting Memory. Other than the statues in front, and a few other ancillary statues by their feet, and a few pictures on the walls, there is nothing in the room. No material objects, and a deep pile carpet that I am half sinking into, half floating on top of, slippers that add to the sensation of being immersed into the room, not touching anything, yet deeply embedded into it, almost snuggled into the fabric of it, as if my self, the self, were dissolving right into the universal solvent, pure and clear and odorless and tasteless and invisible and weightless, neither gas nor liquid nor solid yet all three. As if I were an incense stick incrementally burning off, first into smoke, and then becoming a part of the room. My thoughts, normally bunched together, wrapped in gauze, insistent, urgent, impatient, one moment to the next, living in what I now realize is, in essence, a constant state of emergency (as if my evolutionary instincts of fight or flight have gone haywire, leading me to spend each morning, noon, and evening in a low-grade but absolutely never-ceasing muted form of panic), those rushed and ragged thoughts are now falling away, one by one, revealing themselves for what they are: the same thought over and over again. And once revealed for what they are, these hollow thoughts, these impostors, non-thoughts masquerading as thoughts, memes, viruses, signals fired off, white noise generated by my brain, they are gone.

And it is quiet. Quiet in a way I have never experienced before. As if quiet were a substance, and it were thick, as if that substance were now in my head, filling it like a viscous fluid, some kind of gel. Desire is suffering. A simple equation, and a nice catchphrase. But flipped around, it is more troubling: suffering is desire. Not a unidirectional arrow, not causal, as in, desire leads to suffering. Desire *is* suffering, and therefore, by axiom, suffering *is* desire. *Ting.* A bell rings. I look around for the ringer. A nun, a monk, anyone. But no one seems to have rung the bell. It rang itself. *Ting. Ting. Ting.* The sound is clarifying, purifying, even. It erases every thought from the room, wipes the slate clean. I had been polluting the room with my ideas and they are all gone. And in front of me, I am, for some reason, unsurprised to see my mother, or at least some version of her, standing at the front of the room, just off the center, incense held at the very end, with each hand, between the index and the middle fingers, and hands raised to her forehead, slightly bent at the waist.

My mother, short and compact, the version I knew, my actual mother, was capable of the most unguarded, undisguised love of anyone I ever met. At some point in my loneliness, in the TM-31, I lost my capacity for embarrassment, but my mother never had that capacity in the first place. She would ask for your love in that voice of hers, loud and plangent and raw and seemingly infinite in its neediness, her voice so naked and small and open. It was almost reckless how vulnerable she allowed herself to be; you couldn't help but hate her for doing that to herself, and at the same time hate yourself for giving in to it, and underneath all of that, despite your hate for her, couldn't help but love her. She was not the best person, or the most giving, or the kindest or the most understanding or the most wise. She was jealous and quick to anger and rash and profoundly depressed for my entire life, had been that way since the age of eleven, when her brother had been stillborn, had a life without duration, an open and closed end on the tiny rectangular gravestone, and then when her own mother had died, two days later, of complications, medically, but really, of grief. My mother spent a lifetime grieving and yet she still loved my father with all of her heart: all of it. It was a structure and a vector and a power source that could be directed toward nearly any target even remotely worthy. All of her heart, a meaningless phrase, but correct and precise, too. She used her heart to love him, not her head, and not her words and not her thoughts or ideas or feelings or any other vehicle or object or device people use to deliver love or love-like things. She used her heart, as a physical transmitter of love, and what came out of it was no more voluntary than gravity or time or time travel or the laws of fictional science itself.

My mother finishes her kneeling, and places her incense into a large ceramic urn filled with the accumulated ashes of a thousand, a million, a hundred million earlier sandalwood incense sticks, the dust of past events collected there and made tangible. She pierces the ash pile, fine, talcum-like, soft gray powder, slides her own incense stick down into it, in a perfect vertical, and appears to consider it for an instant, a thin marker, flimsy and direct, an axis, a conduit for prayer, an object and a process that will turn itself from a material thing into the dust around it, transform into visible and invisible substances, will convert itself into heat and smoke to fill the room. The present incense will become the very stuff that props itself up, and allows other, future incense to stand vertically, for a time, each current incense unable to stand alone, only able to perform its function with the help of all other past incense, like time itself, supporting the present moment, as it itself turns into past, each burning stick transmitting the prayers sent through it, releasing the prayers contained within it, nothing but a transitory vehicle for its contents, and then releasing itself into the air, leaving behind only the burnt odor, the haze and residue of uncollectible memory, and at the same time becoming part of the air itself, the very air that allows the present to burn, to combust, to slowly work itself down into nothingness.

She turns to me, and I see at once that this woman is exactly like my mother, but she is not my mother. She is The Woman My Mother Should Have Been.

She is not a could have been. Could have beens are women who are not exactly like my mother. For any given mother, for any given person, there are many could have beens, maybe an infinite number.

No, this woman standing in front of me is something else, she is the one and only Woman My Mother Should Have Been, and I have found her. Looking for my father, I have found this woman, I have traveled, chronogrammatically, out of the ordinary tense axes and into this place, into the subjunctive mode.

This woman turns to me, and she doesn't smile, doesn't really have any emotion in her face at all. This Woman My Mother Should Have Been is like the Platonic ideal of my mother, I realize, and yet at the same time the idea of that angers me. Who made this place? Who is to say that my mother, exactly as she is, my mother-in-fact, isn't the exact perfect version of herself? This woman in front of me, her face clear of any inner turmoil, her face a calm pool of cool water, of equanimity or beatitude or blissful calm. Like my real mother, this woman is a Buddhist, but she follows the teachings, she has spent countless time studying and meditating, slowing her own thoughts down. She has freed herself from her own box, her own tightly circular mental loop, her cycles of highs and lows, anxiety and mania and delayed grief and depression, and in doing so she has become some kind of bodhisattva, has found the peace that my mother always looked for. She is what I knew was always possible for my mom, if all that light inside her could find its way out.

I am standing in front of a complete stranger, a woman whom I have never met, a woman whom I never could have met, in any possible world, through any possible combination of events and chance happenings. A pure hypothetical.

"Do I know you?" she says.

This is my mother.

This is not my mother.

A bell rings.

Ting.

I remember where I've seen those shoes before.

They belonged to my father. Was this where he was? When he was down in the garage by himself, is this what he was building? A machine to take him here?

There are no clocks in this room, because there's no time in this room, because of what this room, this place, this temple is. My mother back on fictional Earth is trapped in a time loop of her own choosing and this woman is her opposite; this Woman My Mother Should Have Been is here now and forever and always and never in this temple of nontemporality.

The room, previously stationary, now feels like it is spinning and vibrating. What is this? Where is this? Is this even a room at all? Am I actually inside of some kind of structure my father built? Am I inside some kind of construct?

The Woman My Mother Should Have Been turns to me, and now she doesn't have such a pleasant look on her face.

"Should you be here?" she says, and I'm about as scared as I can be of a sixty-year-old woman who looks exactly like my mom. What I had perceived as beatific calm has curdled into something sinister, the dead eyes of a prisoner, not a person but an idea of a person, trapped in a temple for all time.

"Just tell me something," I say. "Is he here?"

"Once. A long time ago."

"Where did he go?"

"I don't know. All I know is that he didn't get what he wanted. He thought I was what he wanted, and he just kept saying sorry, over and over again, that this wasn't how he thought it would be, that he had to go."

Her features now soften, ever so slightly, and seemingly without moving a muscle, her aspect has transformed from sinister to forlorn.

"Will you be my family? Will you stay with me here?"

And I'm running, as cruel as it seems, I'm not about to be trapped in this place for eternity with a creepy version of my mother, not really my mother, an abandoned idea, who doesn't have a heart, but is lonely nonetheless. I sincerely hope she finds someone, that she leaves this temple someday and finds some other subjunctively ideal person to spend eternity with, but I've got my own mother to take care of, a flesh-and-blood mother, an imperfect but present tense mother and maybe it's just a rationalization, but for the first time in a while, I am reminded that I am needed, I have obligations to people, as a son, as a guy who fixes time machines, a guy who gets people out of their bad situations. Even if it seems like a dumb back office job and I don't get paid well, people are counting on me, Mom and Phil, and TAMMY and Ed, and if I hadn't gotten a kick in the butt, hadn't run into myself and then shot myself and then opened the book and tried to skip ahead, I might not have ended up here, and seen this, and realized that, in my own way, this is what I was headed for, a life in some dead quiet airless construct my dad built, free-floating in space. I was headed for an entire life spent alone, pitying myself for not being more, ignoring all those people who actually ask me to be more, because they see it in me. I'm running for a door, any door, the door in the northeast corner to the temple. It's locked. I grab the knob and shake as hard as I can. It feels very wrong to do this, in a temple, in a place of silent contemplation, but I think I need to kick the door down. I kick it hard, with the entire bottom of my foot, stomping it, just below the doorknob. This is no ordinary wooden door. Play by the rules, dummy. Who said that? *Ting*. Do I have to spell it out for you? Okay, who is messing with me? *Ting*. Buddha? The Buddha's talking to me? No one is talking to me. I'm talking to myself. I'm not where I think I am. I am somewhere else. This isn't real, but it isn't fake, either. This is not a pleasant universe anymore. *Ting*.

Then I remember: the book is the key. That's what I said to myself. I was giving myself a clue I knew I would need. That's got to be it, right? The book will tell me how to get out of here. I bet there's a secret door! This is so cool! I figured it out! I'm so smart! It's like my very own adventure story. It's even kind of science fictional.

The only problem is that the TM-31 is nowhere to be found. I guess I'm not so smart. I am kind of an idiot. I didn't travel through time to get to this temple. This isn't the past or the future tense, it's the subjunctive. That's why my time machine isn't here.

I cut through the altar area, crossing in front of the large Buddhas, knocking over the huge bowl of incense dust, and now a loose canopy of dust is billowing over the room, and I knock over the stand holding the bell, and that releases a piercing super-*Ting* that cuts right through my eardrums into the center of my head. In the now ash-darkened room, the haze of incense-past literally clouding my vision, I fumble around and try the other door. Locked. It's hard to breathe, I'm coughing, I'm covering my mouth trying not to suffocate, but this soot is filling my nostrils, my lungs. I don't even want to think about where my fake mom is, somewhere behind me, slow-walking like zombies do in the movies. I try kicking this door, try slamming my body into it. Nothing, not even the slightest movement. I'm scared. I'm scared in a Buddhist temple? Maybe the least scary kind of place imaginable? What am I so scared of? Being trapped here? Wanting to stay here? Nothing? Nothingness? Whatever it is, I need to get out. Okay, think. Think. I am an idiot. This is no ordinary wooden door. This is not a physical door at all. It's metaphysical. This is a time barrier or a logic barrier or some other type of barrier that I am not going to be able to break through with my foot or my shoulder. This is a box I am in. I've been getting into and out of boxes all my life. I say box way too much. Even the idea of a box has become a kind of box for me, a barrier against trying to find another word for it, another device. This room I am in was made by my father, is a construct of a life he imagined. He built it with willpower, with the potential energy of forty years of frustration. This place, *in here,* is nothing but a frame of abstraction surrounding empty space and the sublimated intentions of my father. But when he got here, he realized he wanted out. Is that why I'm here now? Did he want to show me this? Is that why I'm in a time loop? Is he asking me to come find him? And as I'm thinking this, ramming my shoulder into the door, it just flies open, and I fly through it, out into nothingness, and then I'm falling and screaming and crying a little bit but mostly just screaming and falling and falling and falling.

Now where am I?

You're in the interstitial matrix that fills up the space between stories.

Who said that?

You did.

I did? Wait, who am I?

You're you.

Oh, good. Thanks. Seriously, where are we?

We're in a shuttle. I'm taking you back to where you were in story space.

(This isn't the TM-31. I'm in some other kind of vehicle. Larger. More room and air and light. The interior is clean, all white and black ceramic. Like Apple designed a spaceship.)

We're on the bus? A space bus?

More like a space elevator. It's called the Bauman transfer system. A vast network of elevators going in all different directions in ten-dimensional space–time. Some are mainlines, some are branches, some are endpoints.

Like a brain.

I guess so.

Or a bus.

If you insist.

(There's soft atmospheric music playing, but otherwise it's quiet. The air-conditioning feels nice. I press my face, still flushed from the heat of the temple, against the cold surface of the window.)

Hello whoever you are?

Still here.

You're retcon, right? This is the retcon shuttle.

You got it.

Can you pick up Ed for me?

Sure. Who's Ed?

My dog.

I don't have any record of a dog.

Technically he didn't exist.

You had a retconned dog for a pet?

Yeah.

(The driver hits a button on his pants. He says, Someone get the dog . . . yeah, I guess we forgot . . . hold on, let me check.)

What does your dog look like?

Kind of a mutt. Brown. Face like mushy oatmeal.

(He relays the description into his crotch. About ten seconds later, the shuttle stops. The door opens. Ed trots in, flops down next to me. I say thanks to the driver, give Ed a few hard scruffs to his furry neck.)

So why am I being retconned? Did I die?

No. You just got somewhere you weren't supposed to go.

My own future? My empty future?

Sure.

What does that mean? That I have no future? That I'm dead?

That's not really for me to answer.

That is annoyingly cryptic.

Thank you. I try.

(We're zipping along through some kind of color space, hurtling through a galactic-scale elevator shaft. Up and down and all around are other elevator shafts, and snaking all around the

Bauman matrix are long tubes of blue and green and red, tendrils and vectors shooting in every direction.

(Out my window I can see the edges of stories as we pass by. Some of them, the space operas, are grand circuses of light. Others are smaller systems, lonesome clusters, dim and muted and private little stories. I had no idea Universe 31 was so big. Bigger than I'd imagined.)

Don't blame yourself.

For what?

For whatever is making you look so guilt-ridden right now.

Who else can I blame?

The guy who gave you the book.

That was myself. My future self.

No it wasn't.

I saw him. He looked exactly like me.

You think what makes you you is what you look like?

No. Yes.

Some guy hands you a book and says this is going to be your story, and you stick to it. You don't know what he's up to or even who he is and you just do what he says just because he looks like you? Listen to me: think about what he asked you to do.

Stick to the story.

And what does the story do?

Makes me skip ahead.

You are a paradox.

I am a paradox.

Your life is one big paradox.

It makes no sense.

Right. Take a guess who I am.

Me.

That's correct.

You don't look anything like me.

Again with the physical universe stuff. What exactly do you think you are? What exactly do you think this place is? You want to tell a story? Grow a heart. Grow two. Now, with the second heart, smash the first one into bits. Gross, right? A bloody pulpy liquid mess. Look at it, try

> to make sense of it. Realize you can't. Because there is no sense. Ask your computer to print out a list of every lie you have ever told. Ask yourself how much of the universe you have ever really seen. Look in the mirror. Are you sure you're you? Are you sure you didn't slip out of yourself in the middle of the night, and someone else slipped into you, without you or you or any of you even noticing?

(Then he hits a button and the entire back wall and every seat behind me in the shuttle blows apart and falls away, leaving me sitting on the rear edge of an exposed relativistic elevator rocketing along the track at, like, one-quarter the speed of light. The heel of my shoe is about an inch from being ground into pure energy and I realize how good the insulation of the shuttlecraft was, and how noisy the real world is outside, how noisy friction is and damage, how it sounds like the cosmic music of the spheres out here but also like all of creation is one active construction site, either construction or demolition or both, and the noise is almost unbearable and the driver isn't shouting, he's still talking pretty softly, and I can hear it in my head, like it's a voice-over.

(The driver grabs me by the neck. Not in a menacing way, just kind of firm. Like I am a child, a baby whose neck he has to support. I don't get a great look at his face, but I realize he sort of resembles me. Just tougher. With a bit more facial hair. Like if I'd had to actually work all my life driving a shuttle bus instead of in a climate-controlled desk job in IT support. He grips my head, pushing it forward, forcing me to look at the outside world.)

Now listen to me. Don't you want to find your father?

(I manage to squeak out an answer.)

Yes.

Then what is the problem?

I don't know.

It's your story, numbnuts.

You think this story belongs to me?

Who else would it belong to? Are you the author of *How to Live Safely in a Science Fictional Universe*? Own up to it.

But that isn't me. That's my future self.

That's my future self, that's my future self. Listen to you. You sound like an idiot. Who do you think you are? Imagine there's a version of you that sees all of it. A version that knows when versions are messing with the other ones, trying to get things off track, trying to erase things. A record of all the keystrokes, the storage of all the versions, partial and deleted and written over. All the changes. All truths about all parts of our self. We break ourselves up into parts. To lie to ourselves, to hide things from ourselves. You are not you. You are not what you think you are. You are bigger than you think. More complicated than you think. You are the only version of you that is you. There are less of you than you think, and more. There are a million versions of you, half a trillion. One for every particle, every quantum coin flip. Imagine this uncountable number of yous. You don't always have your own best interests at heart. That's true. You are your own best friend and your own worst enemy. You can't trust a guy who gives you a book and says, This is your life. He might have been your future, he might not. Only you know how you get there. Only you know what you need to do. Imagine there is a perfect version of you. Out of all the oceans of oceans of you, there is exactly one who is perfectly you. And that's me. And I'm telling you: you are the only you. Does that make any sense?

Not really.

(Then he hits another button and my seat belt whips off and my chair breaks down and just as I'm about to be tossed out of the shuttle, I grab on to the back of the seat in front of me with both hands and just cling for my life.)

Also, your operating system? You should be nicer to her. You love her, right? But you're just kind of mean to her. You should tell her. You should tell her while you have the chance. Now get back to your life and quit being such a whiny little wuss. Be a man. Find your father. Tell him you love him. Then let him go. Then go find your mom and eat her food and tell her it's good.

> Then go and marry that girl you never married. What's her name?
>
> Marie. She doesn't exist.
>
> Neither does your dog, and you love him, right? Anything is possible in this kind of world. You idiot. Go marry Marie. And have a life. And grow a heart. And a pair.

(He gets out of his driver's seat and walks back to my seat and stands in front of me. He slaps me on the face, hard. And then he slaps me on the other side of the face, then he shakes me like I'm a baby, then he kisses me hard on the mouth, which, well, is one of the more disturbing experiences I have ever had, not incest exactly, because I don't know that he actually is related to me, it's just this weird feeling I have, and although the kiss is not, by any means, pleasant, it's also not entirely unpleasant, sort of like when you're a kid and you try to practice on yourself, and for a second you realize, hey, I have breath, and I can smell my own breath and it's not great, and I'm a hot-breathed, mouth-breathing teenager just like all the other hot-breathed, mouth-breathing teenagers, and then he says, I love you, I'm doing this for your own good, and he slaps me one more time for good measure and he hits a button that opens the shuttle door, and shoves me hard out of the shuttle, falling, seemingly without end, and I'm wondering if it's going to be stories, all stories, all the way down, just stories and stories.)

(Outside. Outside the shuttle, outside of my TM-31, no Tense Operator, no grammar drive, no device around me. Out here. Out here, another free body, another part of the broken-down universe. In a moment, I will be falling. In a moment, I will be falling again, but from here, outside, between moments, the TM-31 looks like a phone booth, looks like a shower stall, looks like a cage. From here, I can see what ten years looks like, what a lifetime looks like, spent inside that contraption, my personal mode of propulsion. I can see how I am always in perpetual motion through time, how I can never stop, obsessed with the past, projecting myself into the future, clutching at and always failing to grasp the wisp of now. For a moment, a nonmoment, I can rest, I can clear my head of the noise of existence, from up here, an inch above the time axis, I can look down and see it all laid out, I can just almost start to hear, just start to make out the original sound, the background voice, just start to remember that there was something I've been trying to remember for my entire life, and just when I almost feel like it's starting to come back, just when I've almost got my mind wrapped around it, it's slipping away, it is ending even as it starts, and I know I can't stay in this space here, the next moment will be coming soon, it's here now, and just like that, the memory of the memory of the memory of the sound is gone.)

(And then I'm falling again, Ed is falling right next to me, and we're about smack right on top of my TM-31. I may have broken my sternum. Ow. Manage to pop the hatch, climb back in. Ahh, TAMMY. Ahh, Ed. But then I see it. A corridor of memory. A series of boxes. An endless hallway, a moving diorama, with no ceiling, no fourth wall. It's the father–son axis. If I focus on any one point on the line, I can see the memory clearly. If I relax, and look at it as a whole, it is like a general impression of emotion and color and smells and sounds. We're approaching low, at just the right angle, and I slide into the axis, touching down right in the middle of a memory.)

(module γ)

21

"We're in your childhood," TAMMY says.

Ed senses something different, lifts his head to sniff around.

"Why would shuttle guy drop me off here?" I say.

The view outside the TM-31 is somewhat akin to being inside a very large, very dark aquarium. There are exhibit tanks in every direction, as far as the eye can see, only instead of primordial sharks and bioluminescent jellyfish, all the specimens are me. Me at nine, me at fourteen. It's an after-hours tour of a private museum. We drift past a memory that looks disturbingly familiar to me.

"What are you doin—?" TAMMY starts to ask, trying to interpret the scene. "Oh."

This was that magical, feverish, sweat-soaked afternoon when I'd found my father's stack of old *Penthouses*, taking it all in, trying to store those images, those poses in my memory forever, making the most of my windfall and, apparently, making particularly good use of the July 1988 issue.

"I feel like I understand you better already," TAMMY says.

"Shut up. Shut up."

They're all here in this corridor, good memories and bad, humiliations and accidents and even small victories, each tableau playing out like the movement of silent, benthic sea life, viewed through the viscous and refractive medium of the years in between, in some cases dim and obscured, and others relatively clear, but never completely transparent, at best suggestions, outlines, emotions and echoes, impressions as relived through the deepest and darkest of waters.

There we are, my father and me, in the garage. Here we are, TAMMY and me, we're standing in the garage, invisible to them, watching them through the glass case of memory-proof material along this corridor of the aquarium of the past. It looks and feels as if I am standing in the same room as they are, right in front of my younger self and my father. And it looks as if they are staring, not through me, but right back at me, and with their minds immersed in the theory of time travel and their eyes fixed on the future. Maybe, in a sense, they *are* staring at me. I'd like to imagine that's what my father was gazing at all those times in the garage, his eyes fixed at some point in the middle distance, our future as a family, which is to say, me, and that maybe looking at me, even though he didn't know what he was looking at, was some kind of unconscious inspiration for him, that whatever good feeling he might have had was a reaction to some inexplicable thing he saw in the future. I'd like to imagine even that his ideas, which seemed to come to him from nowhere, could have been just a kind of unknowing comprehension he gained from studying the ghostly contours of my TM-31, that somehow in these future-past-memory interactions he perceived the ineffable, the intangible architecture and shape of an invention he had not yet created, that by some mechanism, in trying to learn something from this private museum of their past, I am helping him, from in here, that in some way his own son was the inspiration for the work he was doing.

I want to believe that I was an idea, a feeling, a longing in my own mind, in the mind of my father.

Or even just a queasiness, an uneasy apprehension, as he stares into my face, as I stare into his.

I can see my younger self now, sniffing the air, just as Ed did, and I realize, finally, what that recurring scent was in my nostrils, the one I always associated with big moments in my life, with the oncoming arrival of something bad, of opportunity mishandled, of lost possibility. I thought it was the stinging odor of failure, like getting punched in the nose, the smell of adrenaline and then embarrassment, some biochemical reaction to learning, time and again, with my father, that the world didn't want our invention.

Now I understand that what I thought was the smell of personal disappointment, the smell of my father's crushed hope, the smell of fear itself, was really just the metallic-tinged ozone vapor coming from the silent exhaust of the TM-31, was just the by-product of time travel, before my father finally escaped his own timeline.

Could that be it? Why I ended up here? To find my father. My father, who managed to escape from his own life. He figured out a way to do something no one else has. Is he the one who can help me get out of this loop?

As we continue to drift along the darkened visitor paths, a particular chain of exhibits softly lights up, as if we're being shown the way by some unseen docent. I point the TM-31 in the direction of the illuminated passage and, silently, our vessel starts to glide down that faintly glowing hallway.

Our first attempt at a prototype was a rickety contraption that my father and I put together over the better part of a summer vacation, during my three months of break before entering middle school. We called the prototype the UTM-1. It was a failure.

My mother and father had been fighting for weeks that summer. The fighting, no matter what it was about, was really about money. Not money itself, as they were both simple in that regard, happy with just enough. The problem was that there wasn't. They fought not about money, but because of the stress from lack of it. They both knew that neither one could do anything about it. They hated themselves for fighting about it. They both tried to hide it from me, but I knew it, and they knew I knew it.

After a particularly bad Fourth of July weekend, my mother had had enough and went to stay with her divorced sister, who lived by herself an hour away, coming back for more clothes every weekend until her closet was almost empty.

I didn't speak to my father for the first couple of weeks after my mother moved out. He came and went, made me dinner or picked up takeout and left it for me on the counter. I took the bus to summer school and when I got home, I watched television all afternoon and night and he never said anything about it. I could hear him in the garage working on the prototype. I still felt bad about the thing I'd said months earlier, about us being poor, but I heard through the walls all those fights, was scared of him, of the voice he used, how such a normally quiet man, gentle even, especially with me, could sound like that when talking to my mom. I was a mama's boy, I guess, and I refused to even go into the garage. Instead, I just sat on the couch and watched *Star Trek* reruns and generally tried to pretend that I had no idea what was going on. I had always been closer to my mother and it had seemed natural to take her side.

I'm standing here in the TM-31, with the cloaking device on, watching my prepubescent self make a sandwich, and I remember this.

I remember that when the fighting started, I would go to my room and close the door and boot up my Apple II-E. It's all coming back now. I see myself working on a program in BASIC, a program for making a spherical object bounce around the screen, like an asteroid in space. I remember that I had gotten the physics right, that was easy. What I couldn't figure out was what should happen at the boundaries, whether the asteroid should, when reaching the edge of the screen, bounce off and reverse direction or keep going right through, around the universe, and then emerge from the other side.

"You were a cute kid," TAMMY says, still giggling about the *Penthouses*.

I see myself pretending to work on the program, pretending even though I was alone, I remember how I would always pretend that I wasn't listening to whatever was going on in the living room, the outpouring of anger in a constant stream, ebbing and rising in waves, punctuated by bursts of outright screaming. I remember how I would sit there thinking, *Who am I trying to fool*, sitting there as if I wasn't fazed by it, every day, for years, ever since I was a small child, as if it had no effect on me, as if it didn't hurt.

I remember thinking all of this and still, and yet, and for whatever reason, continuing to stare at the screen, pretending in my room alone, pretending to myself, as if someone was watching me from above, some semi-omniscient, bird's-eye view observer was watching over me, and what I didn't realize then was that there was an observer, and in fact, it was me, it's me now, looking back at myself from inside this time machine.

TM-31 Recreational Time Travel Device

Standard-issue chronogrammatical vehicle, rated for personal, private use.

Operating system generally reported to be helpful, even if a bit down on itself.

One notable quirk is the word *recreational* in the product's name, which can be read either of two ways, with a hyphen or without, which some have suspected to be an implicit acknowledgment of the fact that "recreational" use of the machine is also, in a sense, "re-creational" use as well.

This idea is consistent with the current understanding of the neuronal mechanism of human memory, i.e., every time a user recalls a memory, he is not only remembering it, but also, from an electrochemical perspective, literally re-creating the experience as well.

22

It was a moonshot, that first trip. It was a soda bottle rocket with a crumpled bottle, it was the Wright brothers' test run, it was a wobbly and earthbound arc, it never got free of the pull of the gravitational present. It lasted all of a minute, less than a minute, maybe fifty-five seconds. Once we climbed in, we couldn't get out, but in the mirror we had placed in the garage (in order to be able to position the cooling element on top of the unit), we could see ourselves, sitting there, we saw what we looked like, a scientist and his know-nothing assistant, two guys in a garage next to a makeshift box, a crate really, with a piece of sheet metal stapled twice as a kind of door, except that it didn't open.

This was how we built it. After fourteen straight days of silence and *Star Trek* reruns, one Saturday morning I went down to the garage and stood there, watching my father work while I ate a bowl of cereal. I couldn't tell if he was mad at me for taking my mother's side, or for not coming down sooner, or something else altogether. I thought I was the one who was supposed to be mad at him. He didn't say anything all day, and we repeated it again the next day.

The next morning, I came down, prepared for a third day of watching him measure things wrong and curse at himself and make trips to the hardware store. This time, though, he handed me a fistful of nails and pointed to a piece of sheet metal leaning against the wall.

"Hammer that," he said, still looking pissed. I did my best to look pissed, too, or as pissed as a ten-year-old can look, but eventually I hammered the nail, and then another, and before long, it was dinnertime. We worked mostly in silence for the next two months, only talking to each other when deciding what to eat for lunch.

By the end of the summer, the UTM-1 was ready. Or so we thought. We stood there in the garage, looking over our contraption, odd pieces of sheet metal sticking out here and there, little gaps where surfaces weren't flush, the general overall slumpy, homemade look to our machine.

"That doesn't look like it's going to work," TAMMY says. "But you guys did a nice job."

She's right. Although we did leave the present moment, and so in that sense we traveled in time, in every other respect we failed. We looped around in a short circuit, but we had no control over the machine. We couldn't get out, we couldn't even stop the thing, it was just a swinging, fishtailing 180, an out-of-control joyride, a minute into the past, and then back, but it took us much longer than a minute to get there, it took us, well, we don't even know how long it took that first time because we didn't know to bring a watch or timepiece. We thought we would appear instantaneously at our destination. We would later find out that even in science fiction, it takes time to travel through time, that there is no instant poof, no shazam, that a vehicle is a vehicle, regardless of what kind of vehicle it is, and that the whole point of transport through some amount of space–time is that it is a physical process. Even if it has metaphysical and fictional implications, it is still a physical process.

This was before, before it all, before we learned all that we would learn in the next few years. Before others would make breakthroughs in chronodiegetics, before I abandoned my studies to become a repairman for a large conglomerate, before we had made our rudimentary maps of the science fictional world. Before he got lost.

"We're doing it," he said.

"The rig is holding up," I said, noting that it was only vibrating slightly. We'd been worried that it might hit a resonant frequency in the acceleration phase and vibrate itself into pieces, just blow itself apart, throwing us into who knows what or where or when.

We were in the garage, with the garage door open, I remember, so I park my TM-31 just outside, behind the basketball hoop and trash cans, so I can watch from here.

"Imagine," my father said, "if we could just stop." If we could just stop at any point in time. If we could stop right now in this subspace, if we got out and well, what?

If we could just stop at any moment in time and change our lives. Rearrange them.

What could we do? What would we do? What would we have done differently? Instead of the ordinary problems of life, the problem of what to do next, of what to do first, of what to do ever, at all, even the smallest step, we would also have the problem of what to do yesterday, of what to do last year, of how to justify anything, ever. There we were between minutes, between moments. We sat there in the crate, unsure of what or when we were, knowing only that we were in transit, in a space between space, a time between times, in some sort of interstitial gap between moments, a subspace occupied by only the two of us.

We sat there for some indefinite and unmeasured period of time realizing our error, our wrongheaded assumption, marveling at what we had learned: time travel takes time. My father was so excited he almost broke our craft, banging on the front door, such as it was, with both fists in celebration of the discovery. Of course, he said, why hadn't he thought of it? Living is a form of time travel. Time travel is a physical process. It has to be. Although we hadn't remembered to bring a timepiece on our maiden voyage, we had remembered to bring a notepad and pencils and even a quarter sheet of graph paper. We thought we would record something, anything, sensory data, our impressions, our physical conditions. But when the time came, we couldn't bring ourselves to move. We just stared at each other. Even in my anger at him, my indignation, I couldn't help but smile, if for no other reason than just seeing my father smile. It was so strange and unsettling to see him like this, to see him happy, strange because I realized I had never seen him like this before, not in our house, not with my mom, not when we were all together in the car taking a drive, never. Not like this. We were doing science. Together. In here, in our little box, in our laboratory separated from the rest of the world. For some period of nontime time or a thousand moments, or maybe just one, we were in there, and he was happy and I was part of it. I remember the goose bumps on my arms and the back of my neck, the excitement at seeing this, at doing something right, for once in our lives, *succeeding*.

Technically, that first time was a failure because we never actually landed, because we could not get the UTM-1 to touch down at our point B and instead, we got swung around in a boomerang path, and ended up back where we started, took a trip through the void and got close enough to see the bumps and rocks and pits and craters and gray, ancient, mysterious surface of the dark side of our own moon, but didn't actually get to walk on it, not that first time. As we approached our destination we realized, too late, that we hadn't actually built a control mechanism that told the machine how or when to stop, realized that, in effect, we had no conceptual landing gear, just before we got bounced back to where we started, there was a moment of suspension, of suspense even, at the top of our arc—a pause during which we were completely stopped, still in free fall but with zero velocity—a brief interval in which we were able to get a good look at our selves, our past selves, just a minute before, before our first flight, before we had gone through all of this, before we had taken that first step, before we knew what was possible and impossible and inevitable, and we looked at ourselves and we could see what was plain, could see what anyone else would have seen, that we looked like a father and a son, we looked like innocents, we looked terrified and stupid and naïve and alive and open to possibility.

Weinberg-Takayama Radius

It is well established within the field of diegetic engineering that a science fictional space must have an energy density at least equal to the unit average level of a Dirac box, multiplied by pi.

However, a new and widely debated conjecture posited by two different researchers, Weinberg* and Takayama,† each working independently and without any knowledge of the other, sets forth the proposition that a universe, in order to sustain the conditions necessary for the development of narrational sustainability, can be no bigger than a certain maximum size, which has, in the literature, come to be referred to as the Weinberg-Takayama Radius (WTR).

* Professor, Center for Research in Advanced Narrative Dynamics, affiliated with the City College of New Angeles/Lost Tokyo-2.

† Professor, Imperial University of Lost Tokyo-1. Also known for his seminal work on the Shen-Takayama-Furimoto Exclusion Principle.

Stated simply, any world with a radius larger than the WTR will eventually dissipate, while any world with a radius smaller than the WTR has the potential, given the right initial conditions, to produce narrational truths in a unified emotionally resonant field.

23

My mother was calling for me when we got back. She had finally come back from her sister's house, pulling up just as my father and I reentered time in the middle of the garage. She was afraid, I could hear it in her voice, how she was on the edge of panic, as she so often was.

On the return landing from our maiden voyage, the machine had fallen apart. In fact, it didn't even make it back to our original starting point, reentering in a ball of heat sometime during the minute we had traveled over. We crash-landed somewhere in that lost minute, which was a good thing, maybe a necessary thing, since it meant that there weren't two sets of us in existence at that moment, and going forward, but it did confuse things.

I didn't understand it then, but now, watching her from up here, in the minute before we emerged, I see that she'd just gotten back, her sister was dropping her off, and as she struggled to get the broken and mismatched luggage out of the trunk I could see the look on my mom's face, a look I recognized, half of her terrified of losing control and blowing up at my father, half of her hoping he might, contrary to all previous behavior, be waiting for her with unguarded love in his eyes.

What she probably hadn't been expecting to see was a big hole in the middle of the cement in the garage floor, and half of the tools in the garage singed by a fire our machine had apparently ignited on launch, and most of the ceiling not so much singed as scorched, and a stack of old newspapers in the corner burning a nice, healthy orange flame near cans of old cleaning solution.

There she is, falling over her luggage, into the trash cans, screaming for us, wondering where we were, assuming the worst, as she always did, assuming catastrophe, just utter unimaginable worst-case disaster for our family, how in her state of anticipatory panic she had dropped a cake she had bought from the grocery store on the ground and her stocking had a run in it and her hair was a little crazy.

And now here we come, my younger self and my dad, our machine blinking into existence, and from this vantage point I can see what I didn't see the first time, how I look to my mother as she watches me, climbing out of the machine, a little, skinny-armed boy, her boy, I can see how my dad looks to her, still in our device, smiling, and how stupid the machine looks as it falls apart, just as Dad is climbing out. Now I see why she is crying. My father doesn't. He hardens his face against her, against the situation, which normally would bother me but this time I don't understand why she is crying, either, and so I kind of harden my face a little, too, in my ten-year-old way, and she notices this, I think, she is holding me and getting me all wet and smeared with makeup and tears, and I am looking at her in her sweater with cats on it, thinking, *Pull it together, please, Mom, just for once, why can't you let Dad see the side of you I see, not always like this,* and she looks up at me and I feel like a miniature version of my father and then she starts crying even harder, and I wonder if she even understands why she is crying. In school our class has been reading a story about a woman who falls into a hole and cannot get out and everyone in the town tries to help her out, but they can't seem to pull her out and at the end, they all walk away one by one, and this is before I start to see commercials on television, with people staring out rain-streaked windows, commercials advertising medicine for some kind of condition, of what, I am not sure, a disease of the brain? Of the heart? Of the soul? This is before I learn to put my mother in that diagnostic box and label it, keep her in there, tidy and categorized, long before any of that, when I can still see her crying as what it is, in its raw, unnamed form, jagged, knife-like sobs, pure and intense, wonder why it is so powerful, why she needs to do it, why it bothers my father so much. I can still wonder if it might be a kind of bridge between what is and what could have been, what is and what isn't anymore, what is and what never was, and that wouldn't make the crying any less awful but it would make a kind of sense.

TAMMY makes her pixels into a sloppy, runny-nosed face. She loads her crying subroutine and tries it out, snuffling a little bit to herself, for my mom, I guess.

Then Ed farts and it is not good. TAMMY's still crying but starts to giggle, and I'm gagging a little, and then TAMMY starts laughing so hard she almost crashes herself. Ed saves the day again.

24

A call comes in from Dispatch.

"What the hell?" I say.

"It's Phil," says TAMMY. "You should let it go to voice mail."

"I know, right? He's calling me? Now? What a dick."

"No, it's not that. You're stuck in a time loop."

"That's what I'm saying. I'm taking a personal day, dude. Jerk boss. I'm going to tell him off."

"No. Do not pick up that phone. I'm not talking about him being a jerk. I'm saying: you are stuck in a time loop. If you take that call, then you always took that call. You always take that call. It's got to be self-consistent with the rest of this. If you pick up that phone, it's just one more thing that we'll have to do again. And who knows what complications it leads to."

"Holy Heinlein," I say. "What would I do without you?"

"Cease to exist," she says, allowing herself a little smile.

I was sixteen when my father had his next breakthrough.

TAMMY takes note of my postpubescent form, notes the disparity from my present-day physique.

"Hey, you used to have muscles," she says, surprised.

"Shut up. Just shut up."

By this time in our prototype numbering scheme, we were up to the UTM-21. We had crashed the UTM-3, the UTM-5, the UTM-7, 9, 11, and so on, each odd-numbered model failing in some new, unexpected way. We'd spent hours, years in here, trying to improve our idea, but what was happening was simple: we kept crashing. It was easy to figure out what. What we couldn't figure out was why.

My father was at the chalkboard.

"Pay attention," he said. "We can figure this out. We have to figure this out."

As much as anything else, he was trying to convince himself. I was ready to quit, to go upstairs, to leave the house, to be a man of my own. Or to just be a teenager. Anything else but watch my father any longer. I'd grown up. Didn't he see that? I was already taller than him, had been for a couple of years, was too tall for my family. We'd been doing this for so long, since I was ten, and we'd had some good times, but where was this all going? What was his plan for this, us, our family?

"More research," he would say. "We need more data points."

His trajectory at work had already become apparent, had started to move sideways, and my mother, after a good year, was in a holding pattern herself. In some ways she'd started to regress, even picking up new habits, new ways of tearing my father down, tearing herself down, found a way to cry harder, more jagged, more raw. She would disappear into her room some Friday nights and not come out the whole weekend, and then emerge, Monday morning, and everything would be okay again. Things were livable, were bearable, but at sixteen, I felt old, I felt tired of this, of prototypes and going sideways, of back and forth, I felt mediocre, I could see where this was headed and I wanted to escape my own future.

At some point in that year together, the last year we were recognizable as a family, my father had started to sound different. He still spoke in the same manner, gruff, as if I were always on the verge of annoying him, but there was a subtle change in what he said, in the questions he asked. I could hear, within each one, another question curled up, folded up inside, hidden from me, perhaps not fully intentionally placed in there by him. They had gone from tests, games, teaching, to something else. Something like wondering. Something harder, more genuine. Asking.

"Do you think there's something wrong?" he asked me once while I had my head buried in a control panel.

"Niven ring is cracked. We'll need to fuse it shut."

"No, not that. I mean with the theory."

"I don't understand."

"The theory. My theory. Is it, did I take a wrong turn somewhere in the equations? Did I get it wrong?"

My father had begun asking my opinion about the world. He was admitting, in his way, what he didn't know, what confused him, what frustrated him in this country, at work, in this town, both close and far from the center of everything. He was asking me if I was ready to be part of our family, ready to help him, ready to be a numerator.

I remember feeling small, unprepared, like I had to help him, feeling like how in the world could I possibly help him. I was angry at him for asking, sorry for him for having to, angry at myself for not being more prepared, for not being the gifted kid he once thought I was, for not being who he had hoped I would be.

The house became charged, a field of static potential energy, a kind of vectorless disappointment, a field of invisible isovoltaics, lines with arrowheads pointing in minute directional indicators, a bogglingly complex arrangement of single-point losses, the fine-toothed, fine-pixeled array, the heat map of a thermodynamic system whose ending was already foretold in the current steady state.

It wasn't until well after midnight that it happened, by that point, we'd been staring at the chalkboard for nine and a half hours. It was cold, but to concede that to my dad would have brought I'm not sure what kind of reaction, so I just kept my mouth shut and my eyes focused on our neighbor, across the street, who was my age, kissing her boyfriend good-bye for what seemed like the entire night.

My father was undeterred. He stood there, staring at the math, working it over and over again. Theta and nu, sigma and tau. The tau doesn't modulate, he said. "Does that make any sense to you?" he said, pointing to a board full of differential equations.

"I don't even know what I'm looking at."

"Oh yeah," he said. "Sorry. It says that we are colliding with other objects."

"Maybe we are," I said.

"That's impossible," he said. "Unless . . ."

He paused, staring off into space, when something hit him, something real but invisible. I could see it, the impact, and his face opened up, his eyes widened, his jaw dropped. So this was what he worked for, all this toiling in the garage: a moment like this. It might come once a year, or once a decade. He yelped in pain or joy. And he hugged me. He threw chalk up in the air and clapped his hands and made a huge cloud of white chalk dust and he jumped up and down and whooped and just generally looked silly. So this was what he loved: science. So this was what it looked like: my father, happy.

Then he erased the whole board and picked up a new piece of chalk and started scribbling, chalk flying, breaking the chalk, yelping in exclamation every minute or so, pounding on his own head in excitement, and when he stopped after what felt like hours, covered in white, his fingers raw, hair matted against his face, sweat dripping from his ears, in his eyes, he said, You did it, you figured it out, son, we are crashing. We are crashing into time machines everywhere. He pointed to the board, an illegible tangle of equalities and inequalities and infinities and asymptotes, and he started to explain, shouting, his voice hoarse.

I don't remember everything he said, exactly, but I remember the feeling, the idea, where he was going with it, the idea that our equations had been too simple, too naïve, that we had been assuming a time machine was some kind of specialized object, that we only had to solve for an isolated variable, when in fact a time machine was just a special case. He said: A house can be a time machine. A room. Our kitchen, this garage, this conversation, anything can be a time machine. Just sitting there, you are. So am I.

Everyone has a time machine. Everyone *is* a time machine. It's just that most people's machines are broken. The strangest and hardest kind of time travel is the unaided kind. People get stuck, people get looped. People get trapped. But we are all time machines. We are all perfectly engineered time machines, technologically equipped to allow the inside user, the traveler riding inside each of us, to experience time travel, and loss, and understanding. We are universal time machines manufactured to the most exacting specifications possible. Every single one of us.

TM-31 calibration protocol

To calibrate the unit to your specifications, follow these steps:

1. Attach the sensors to your fingertips.
2. Put on the percepto-visual mind-output capture goggles.
3. Lie back.
4. Look at the world.

The process takes forty-three to forty-four seconds, depending on factors such as body mass, natural hair color, and degree of self-knowledge.

When the calibration is complete, your vehicle will have the same limits that you do.

You can't build a car that violates the laws of physics. Same goes for a time machine. You can't go just anywhere, only to places it will let you go. You can only go to places that you will let yourself go.

25

I am seventeen years old. My father will turn forty-nine next week. This is the best day of his life.

If a life is an arc, and an arc has a high point, then that high point is today.

We are in the car driving to the good side of town.

"You look nervous," TAMMY says.

"This is a big day," I say to TAMMY.

We're going to meet an important man, the director of research at the Institute of Conceptual Technology, a gleaming black building, behind gates, that sits on top of University Road, up the hill half a mile above town, where they worked on the hard problems. The big ones, like how to keep paradox from destroying the sci-fi world. They were the people my father aspired to be, this man in particular, they lived the lives he longed for, they drove up to those gates every morning and checked with the security guard and showed their ID badges and the gates opened for them, and they drove behind them, up into the compound, the castle of secrets and ideas that only a hundred people in the world knew about, ideas that only a dozen people understood.

Today is the day, that one glorious day in my father's life. After waiting half a lifetime, half a career, his moment. Today is the day they come calling for him. They, the world, the outside institutional world of money and technology and science fictional commerce. I remember the call. Sometime after our first wobbly orbit and before he was completely sure he knew what he was doing (or rather, before he realized he would never be completely sure about what he was doing), someone had taken notice. They found him, the military-industrial-narrative-entertainment complex, and they wanted to hear his idea. This is the day he has dreamed about, the day even I have dreamed of. This is the day that has hung over our house, in the air, for years, the cloud of a shared dream. If a lifetime in the end is remembered for a handful of days, this is one of them.

After his day of revelation in the garage, he had been back on the upswing, as a scientist, even as a burgeoning entrepreneur. Even as a husband. It was all moving up: meaning, success, our story. For a while here, it looked like we were going to make it. Whatever it is. Whatever making it is. He was going to make it, our family was, my mother and father were going to make it. The world was coming to him, finally. He had made a noise, and the world heard him, and the world was coming. And just as he had always imagined, it was coming with money. Or more accurately, the promise of money. More than money. Prestige. The promise of prestige and a sense of mystery about him, a sense of intellectual mystery that would surround him, inventor, pioneer, scientist. He imagined the prospect of seeing his name in trade journals, rivals and admirers whispering about what he was working on, his method of working, how he got his ideas. He imagined how the people at work would react when he quit, when a month after he quit they realized what they had let slip away, how they could never afford him now, how they had ignored him all those years, put him in the cubicle, let him inch upward, never seeing the quality of his ideas.

I am excited. I am hopeful. I know how this all turns out, what happens after today, and still I feel hopeful, looking at myself, remembering how it felt to feel that way. He talks about getting something nice for my mother, about wanting to get a bigger house for us.

We're meeting at a local park, the one in the center of the good side of town, with good photorealistic grass and globally rendered ambient sunshine, the kind they only have in this part of the city. This side is where the private high school is, the school our school doesn't play any sports against, because the private school is too small. They don't even field a full football team. They have a debate team. In the student parking lot for the school, the cars are bigger, and nicer, and in that part of town the houses are bigger, the sidewalks cleaner, the air purer, the kind of upper-middle-SF neighborhood where the residents took pains to create a picturesque and manicured reality.

"He looks," TAMMY says, unsure of the word she is searching for.

"Happy."

"No," she says. "Not that."

So often on drives like this my father was auto-dislocated, there but not there. Early on, by the age of nine or maybe seven or even five, I could already see, had already developed the faculty of chronodiegetical observation, a sensitivity to time–space auto-dislocation, to very subtle shifts in the manifold, the vector field of conscious attentiveness in the interior space of our family car.

But on this day, this momentous day for him, I felt him fully there with me in our Ford LTD station wagon, not even embarrassed about our car, which gave me, for just those few minutes, the ability to not be embarrassed about it, either.

We arrive first, park in the spot nearest the baseball diamond, open the back of the station wagon.

Careful, he says, unclear if it's for me or to himself or to no one in particular.

In the time it took to pull in, park, and get out of the car, he's gone from happy to stressed out.

He is doing his jaw-clenching thing, really working it. It almost looks painful. We move the machine gingerly, taking little baby steps the whole way from the parking lot to the baseball diamond, which seems, under the powerful sunshine of this foreign neighborhood, like a near-infinite distance. Dad doesn't say anything, just grunts and walks a little too fast, and we have to stop twice because I'm losing my grip. We're standing there in the sun and I notice, maybe for the first time, that my father is a man. A human man. His physicality, his sweaty person-ness.

He has very black hair, a whole head's worth, more, thick and strong-looking and so black that it occurs to me, not then, but now, that he must actually dye it. My father is old. Not old, not even fifty, still strong in the forearms and calves and his back and on most days, he has more energy in his compact, half-century-old frame than I do in my brooding, sulky seventeen-year-old clothes hanger of a body. He parts his hair to the right and combs the sides back, and a trickle of sweat is edging downward from his hairline on the left side of his face, where his glasses, nearly square-framed (sort of a top-heavy trapezoid shape popular with engineers), gray and metallic, where the arm of his glasses presses against the skin of his temple, and I wonder why his glasses are fitted so tight, why he wouldn't have gotten a better pair, and I remember that he picked those off the rack at the store between the postal boxes pickup station and the ice cream place, and that he picked them because they were the cheapest frames and fully covered by insurance.

His skin is taut, good living, no drinking, little meat, mostly vegetables and rice and fish and a lot of exercise in the garage and the yard and around the house and just generally being a grinder, being the kind of person who sweats because he has to, not for fun, the only real vice a very occasional cigarette snuck in the backyard after I'd gone to bed. I caught him once, not on purpose, I was going to the fridge late one night and saw him sitting there in the backyard, in one of our white plastic lawn chairs, looking up at the sky, and he didn't even try to hide it, really, just put his hand down, but I could see the ribbon of smoke from behind him, rising and breaking up into a cloud by his head, he just looked at me and didn't smile, but didn't give me a face that he would normally give, it was like he'd taken off his father mask for the night and, for once, for just this moment, wasn't going to put it back on, was going to let me see him without it, and I saw a face I didn't recognize, crushed, drained, I saw defeat, I saw even a kind of resignation. But that isn't how he looks now.

The director pulls up in a Town Car. We're standing there, a little off the rubber, between the pitcher's mound and second base. My father is so nervous it almost looks like he wants me, a senior, a kid, a B student in physics, wants me to talk for him. The director is a balding man with a severe set of eye sockets and a neatly knotted tie, a big knot, the kind neither my father nor I ever seemed to be able to do, wide and dimpled and symmetrical. His shirt has cuffs that are a different color from the rest of the shirt, except for the collar. My father's shirt is buttoned up, he doesn't have a pocket protector, but he has his shirt tucked into brown slacks one-eighth of an inch too short for his five-foot, four-inch frame, he looks neat and competent and like a perfect engineer. The director extends his hand to my father, nods at me politely, and then, to my surprise, shakes my hand as well.

"We have some ideas," he says to my dad. "We have ideas about your idea." And I realize, uh-oh, before any of it has even started: none of this is going to work out. Just the way the man is talking, standing, his tie, his cuff-linked shirtsleeves, his clear, authoritative manner of speaking, the way he manages to treat my father with deference, with respect, while at the same time giving off the impression of doing us a favor, like he is the one who is offering us a chance, because he is. Like we are the bumbling amateurs who have stumbled on a rare coin in a boot in our attic, or had the dumb luck to dig up a Precambrian fossil in our little backyard. All of our plans, our notebooks, our three-ring binders with the college-ruled eight-and-a-half-by-eleven composition paper, all of our one-centimeter-square light green graph paper, every open-ended project, what had it amounted to? Just one success, one partial success. Sure, we are here, this man came to see us, but in the grand scheme of things, we are minor. We are, but for one possible exception, failures. This man has patented world-changing technology, has created whole industries at his desk, in his lab, this man does more real science in a good month than we've done in almost ten years, has thrown away better ideas than the best we will ever come up with.

"He seems . . . ," TAMMY starts, still unsure of what she's thinking, and now watching, with her little pixilated face, as intently as I am.

And what had we done? We had plugged away, scrap by scrap, paper scrap and metal scrap, we had plied our trade, journeymen, not even a trade, we had our little hobby, and now we were a curiosity. That was it. We have still never gotten anything right. We are dreamers who have stuck around long enough to have one semi-interesting dream. This is not going to work out. I know it on some level. This is us, this is us in relation to the world. If I could draw it, it would look like my father and me very small, world very big, with a barrier between us and the world. We are too slow, too methodical, too square, too plodding. We are naïve. This is how it has always gone with us.

This man, though, this man knows things. He is a gentleman, he makes me feel small, makes my father look small, makes our family seem tiny, in his formality, his politeness, his kindness, even. He can afford to be kind, he can afford something I have never experienced until now (something I will soon learn about at the university, where some of my upper-middle-class classmates, with their strangely nice bedsheets and faster computers and discreetly expensive clothes tossed casually over the chair or in piles on the floor, so different from my prepressed, store-label khakis, folded in my half-empty drawer, how these classmates took me seriously, were nice to me in a way that got under my skin, how at ease they seemed, at ease in the science fictional world, in this science fictional country, how perfectly nice and respectful they were to me, asking me where I was from, and not meaning my parents, how they had etiquette and manners and even political sensitivities, and yet I could never put a word to it, to what bothered me about their niceness, an idea to it until, in freshman literature, second semester, I stumbled across the phrase *noblesse oblige,* and immediately flushed with embarrassment right there in class, blood hot in my temples and ears, flushed red in the face at the words, as if a joke, as if it were all a joke, one big joke on me and my dad for all these years, a joke I wish I'd learned long ago), this director of research, this man on top of the profession, he can afford to take us seriously. He has a kind of practical intelligence, savvy. My father and I lack resolve, self-confidence, the willingness to impose ourselves on others, on a situation, on a set of circumstances, to step on things, to willfully forget our deficiencies, we are too self-aware to turn off that nagging internal critic, editor, co-author, to suspend our understanding that we are trying to do what we really have no business doing. We aren't like the director. This man is someone for whom the world isn't a mystery. The world is a boulder, but it has levers and he knows when and where and how to apply just the right amount of force, and it moves for him, while my father and I, pushing up against it, don't have any angle, any torque, no grip or traction or leverage. My father thinks success must be in direct proportion to effort exerted. He doesn't know where or how to exert the least amount for the most gain, doesn't know where the secret buttons are, the hidden doors, the golden keys. He thinks that, even if you have a great idea, there have to be trials and tribulations, errors and failures, a dark night of the soul, a slog, a time in the desert, a fallow period, a period of quiet, a period of silent and earnest and frustrated toiling before emerging, victorious, into the sunshine and acclaim. My father makes to-do lists, makes plans, makes business plans. This is how he starts, always with a blank sheet of graph paper. We make bullet points. We identify the key areas we need to research further. We try to figure out how to research those areas. We work in a vacuum. We work in his study. We ponder. We stare at our feet. We stare at the ceiling. We talk to each other, create a world, create a tiny, artificial, formal space, on a blank sheet of paper, where we can imagine rules and principles and categories and ideas, all of which have absolutely nothing to do with the actual world out there. We don't actually do anything. He writes things down, he crosses them out, he goes back and starts again. The world has always felt just out of his reach. The world of commerce, of men taking advantage of situations, of competition, of sharp practice and words and elbows and speed, a world that was too fast for him. And yet my father will never stop trying, my father will go on for years after this day, thinking that if he just reads another book, just figures out the key, the secret, the world, the world of science fiction with its promise and possibility, will open up to him, to us, for us.

Could this be the time? Is this the day that happens? My father is talking slowly. The director asks him questions, looking at the machine, standing off to a distance, trying to study it while listening to my dad. I can't tell what he's thinking, it could be that he can already see some kind of problem, some wires crossed, misplaced, some fundamental flaw in its architecture. Or maybe he's just listening to my dad talk slowly, too slow, that's always been a problem for him, I've even tried to hint at it, and the way the director is looking at my dad, a little quizzically, a bit puzzled, patiently but like that patience will not last forever, it just seems impossible that we will actually pull this off. And yet, there he is, he's still asking questions and my dad is answering them and the director is nodding, and even smiling, even squinting his eyes trying to visualize something my father is saying to him, and somehow, even though I already know what is going to happen, I can't help feeling excited, I can see that my dad is feeling the same thing, too. If a lifetime in the end is remembered for a handful of days, this is one of them. This is a day when my father is everything he has always wanted to be. Everything I have always wanted him to be. Everything he normally isn't. But maybe this is who he really is, maybe we go through life never actually being ourselves, mostly never being ourselves. Maybe we spend most of our decades being someone else, avoiding ourselves, maybe a man is only himself, his true self, for a few days in his entire life.

As I watch my father talk about his project, our project, I stop recognizing him. He is saying the right things in the right way and now I am starting to feel ashamed for ever doubting him, for the way I had ducked my head at the director when he shook my hand in a gesture of unconscious, preemptive apology for taking up the man's time, which we presumably did not deserve. I feel ashamed of it, of myself, ashamed for all the head ducking I've done in my life, literal and otherwise, for the way I go through life apologizing for my father, for myself, for our family. I feel angry at myself for not having realized all this years ago, for all the wasted opportunities, avenues that I had looked down wistfully thinking, If only we were more prepared, more savvy, if only we had our acts together. If only we weren't ourselves, could somehow be better versions of our selves. I am angry at myself, realizing how many hundreds or thousands of instances in which my father must have looked at me, his son, looked in my eyes to see if I believed in him, if I had any more optimism than he did, if I saw the world just as he did, or if instead he had imparted his sadness and feeling of incompleteness on me. I have let him down. I have let him down countless times. I am seventeen years old, and even then I know that seventeen years old is not very old, but it is old enough to have disappointed him, old enough to have been able to help him, and then chosen not to, it is old enough to be a coward, to have not protected him when you could have, even should have. Seventeen years old is not old, but it is old enough to have hurt your father.

And now, here I am, feeling proud, feeling guilty about feeling proud, feeling stupid about feeling guilty about feeling proud because I should be in the moment, trying to help him, instead of wallowing in my own guilt over my belated and unearned and undeserved pride. My father explains his theory, which, to this day, I still wonder if he made up on the spot. He is doing it, he is pulling it off. I am his son. This man has asked to come see us, not the other way around, and we are worth his time.

"The acquisition of tensed information," my father explains, to both of us listening and possibly to himself as well, "that is the key here." How do we find out about information at a time other than our present? This was the key insight I had in my laboratory one night (me: you did?), while looking at my son working on the bench test (me: are you talking about me?).

The director breaks in to ask a question. What does any of this have to do with time travel?

A good question, my father counters, sounding uncharacteristically polished. The director is even more hooked. My father explains that humans, because of our memories, are good at perceiving intervals of time. That we all have some intuitive understanding of scope and scale and size and units and structure and sequence, an innate ability to organize and process information about such intervals.

"The key question of time travel," my father says, "is this: How do we know what it means to perceive an event as presently occurring, rather than as a memory of a past event? How can we tell present from past? And how do we move the infinitesimal window of the present through the viewfinder at such a constant rate? Why can we see a faraway snow-tipped mountain range, or a jet taking off, or the moon, or the sun, or stars, and not an event that took place a moment ago, let alone a month ago, a year, thirty-three years ago?"

The director is nodding and smiling and my father is smiling a little and I'm allowing myself a smile.

"Maybe it's because we need to be able to do so, for our survival. For food-gathering purposes, for outrunning the saber-toothed tiger, for jumping across jagged rocks in a rushing river, to care for our crying infant, we need to focus, we need to know what is going on now. That is to say, our physical ability to understand time has been honed by evolutionary pressures to select for traits useful for survival, in all aspects, and time perception is no exception or special case or even magical or mysterious case."

My father looks at me and smiles when he says this next part. "Which is where I started to have hope. If there is no absolute logical reason why we could not experience the past just like we experience the present, perhaps we can untrain, or perhaps retrain, ourselves to have such a capacity. Maybe some lobe in our brains, buried in a fold given over to language or calculation of differential survival rates or logic, maybe within that brain structure lies the long-dormant (for our species at least) ability to experience time in a different way."

The director here raises his eyebrows at the suggestion that my father seems to be making: time travel is not a technology built outside, with titanium and beryllium and argon and xenon and seaborgium, but rather it is a mental ability that can be cultivated.

"We have evolved to have current, temporally proximal beliefs about the world," my dad says, "which is to say local-scale accurate beliefs, but perhaps in this case, local-scale accuracy is not the only goal worthy of obtaining. We perceive the present, but we remember the past. The converse is not possible. We obviously cannot remember the present. Or can we? Déjà vu. What does that feel like? It is the oddest experience, one everyone has had, one that is commonly described as a feeling of certainty that one has experienced just this exact experience before. Which in itself is quite strange, the idea that one could have an identical experience, down to the last detail, down to the internal qualia, the exact interior frame of mind, emotions, a frame of consciousness duplicated with startling exactitude, that would be unsettling enough. And yet it's stranger than that."

And I know what he means. I'm standing here, on this baseball field. I have done this before, but not exactly.

"We experience the present and remember the past," Dad continues. "We can't remember the present, except what is déjà vu but a memory of the present? And if we can remember the present, why can't we experience the past? What kind of machine is this? This machine, what my son and I have built, this is a perception engine, and it works in your mind as much as anywhere else."

TAMMY says she's figured it out, what that look is that my father has, and I tell her to shut up, because truly today for once in all of our days, it is going great, just great, really great, and for a brief moment at the top of the arc, we weigh nothing and it seems like maybe the arc wasn't an arc after all, but a straight shot, up to where we have been looking, not aiming, afraid to even admit our aim could ever be so high, but looking, secretly, at a different trajectory of life, and in that moment I think maybe we might have escaped the pull of our lives, of our story, of the chronodiegetic field, of the forces of physics in this science fictional universe, the path and shape and limitations, the constraints, invisible, intangible, but more real than anything, the parabolic track we are on, the equation floating next to our function, I think maybe my father has done it, and then slowly, over days and weeks and months, slowly over a year, and also all at once, in that hot moment at the park on the grass with the day brightening and the air heating up, I begin to realize that this feeling is a familiar one, one I have felt before.

"He looks like he already knows it won't work," TAMMY says, finally, just at the moment I see it, in his face, see what she's talking about, see that it's not the freedom of escape I am feeling, rather it's the weightlessness that is, in fact, the telltale sign of inescapability, that brief instant being the necessary top, the maximum, the defining characteristic of an arc, that weightlessness is really the last second, tenth of a second, the last few milliseconds we will enjoy as we start to come down from the top.

Failure is easy to measure. Failure is an event.

Harder to measure is insignificance. A nonevent. Insignificance creeps, it dawns, it gives you hope, then delusion, then one day, when you're not looking, it's there, at your front door, on your desk, in the mirror, or not, not any of that, it's the lack of all that. One day, when you are looking, it's not looking, no one is. You lie in your bed and realize that if you don't get out of bed and into the world today, it is very likely no one will even notice.

Hitting the peak of your life's trajectory is not the painful part. The painful day comes earlier, comes before things start going downhill, comes when things are still good, still pretty good, still just fine. It comes when you think you are still on your way up, but you can feel that the velocity isn't there anymore, the push behind you is gone, it's all inertia from here, it's all coasting, it's all momentum, and there will be more, there will be higher days, but for the first time, it's in sight. The top. The best day of your life. There it is. Not as high as you thought it was going to be, and earlier in your life, and also closer to where you are now, startling in its closeness. That there's a ceiling to this, there's a cap, there's a best-case scenario and you are living it right now. To see that look in your parents' faces at the dinner table at ten, and not recognize it, then to see it again at eighteen and recognize it as something to recognize, and then to see it at twenty-five and to recognize it for what it is.

The worst part of the drive back from the park was not that we didn't talk, that would have been okay, fine, that would have been better than what happened, which was my father pretending to be happy. He turned on the radio, he asked what song I wanted to listen to, he asked me about the song on the radio, he even tried, and this is the worst part, to sing along. I knew what was happening, but he kept it up for long enough and was singing and smiling all crazy enough that I wondered if he'd burst some pipe in his head, if the pressure and force of the crushing blow had damaged his own emotional machinery.

There's my dad, pretending to be okay, pretending he isn't reeling, hasn't just had the wind and life and fight knocked out of him, hasn't just had something inside of him, the last bit of anything delicate inside, smashed into a couple hundred tiny pieces.

I see myself staring straight ahead at the road, trying hard not to look over at my father, already replaying the events in my head.

"So," the director had said, "only one thing left to do. Fire it up."

My dad and I look at each other. As agreed, he's the one to get in. He takes off his suit jacket, hands it to me, and I lay it over my arm, hoping to impart some ceremony to the moment. My father has on short sleeves under his jacket, and if the director thinks it odd, he doesn't show it. Dad looks small in there, his shoulders a little slumped. He nods and I close the hatch.

I am watching my self thinking, *We should have stayed in our garage*. I am watching him think that and I am thinking it myself now. Why couldn't we have just stayed in there, in our laboratory, our space. We should have stayed where we were safe. Maybe things would have been different, maybe the thing would have worked, the piece of junk, maybe I wouldn't have had to watch my father sweat and strain and stand there awkwardly, trying everything for what is probably eight, ten minutes but feels like my entire life. It is, it was, it has been my entire life, my father's life, too, those few eternal unending merciless minutes dragging and stretching on in silence, the director ever the gentleman, unwaveringly polite, which makes it worse, polite until the end, the etiquette of a situation like this unclear to me and to him, as we stand there for the awful duration of this stretch of time on what was supposed to have been the best, brightest-shining hour of my father's story, through the first phase of let me try this, it must be that, simple fix, to the heh heh, that's funny, this never happens in our lab (me knowing, and hoping the director doesn't know, even as we are failing, hoping that the director at least can't imagine what my father means when he says "our lab," our messy garage in our messy house, with our scribblings everywhere, our workshop with the random objects everywhere, a basketball, an old yearbook of mine, a rusted fork sitting on top of a tray full of assorted screws and nails and bolts, bad tools, bent and tired, decade-old oil stains under our LTD wagon, the cat's litter box stinking the whole place up), then on to the stage of oh what were we thinking that we could pull off something like this, the stage of self-questioning, asking me, Hey son, do you remember if I checked this or that, a stalling tactic, a misdirection, of me realizing then how good a man my father was and is, how, even in his worst moment, he would never, ever, in a million years blame me for something, even if it was my fault, not like this, not in front of this stranger, even if it was my fault, and who knows, it probably was, I wasn't half the scientist my father is or was, I never could have been, of me realizing my father would have never even thought about trying to pin it on me, though he could have, it would have been easy enough, and I wish I could freeze time right then and there forever, wish I could hold that knowledge forever, the realization that, even in the gut-turningly horrible awkwardness of that situation, the absolute low of all lows, in the most desperate minute of this hour of his greatest embarrassment and unexplained bad luck and, yes, failure, even though he could be absent and fuzzy and unlocatable and clench his jaw at me and always be disappointed in me and use silence as a form of cruelty to me and my mother, despite all of that, my father would always protect me against the world, would always stand between the world and me, would always be a buffer, a protective covering, a box for me to hide in.

And then finally comes the last stage, we can almost go home now, in the hot car and then the cold garage and the even colder house, can almost go back into our box and hide, but not before a couple more minutes of head-scratching, my father actually standing there scratching his head with his hand, his small hand, strong and with well-defined veins, but still small, how the smallness of his hand, of his entire height just hit me, the image of him looking like an immigrant, like a bewildered new graduate student in front of the eminent professor, a small man with a small hand in a large foreign country, not so much scratching his head as just pushing his hand up against it, as in, Oh what's happened, oh why now, why like this, betrayed by his own invention, the anguished embarrassment made that much worse by all of his soliloquy, by all of his grandstanding theoretical monologue that preceded it, and worst of all, because he has just finished explaining how his machine is an idea, is a device of the mind, this failing not being just a fluke, not just a piece of bad mechanical luck, but an actual failure of his own mind, his own concept. The silence is just unbearable now, and to make things worse, now kids are starting to appear at the edges of the diamond, parents pulling up with coolers, bags of bats, the slapping of mitts, the thwock of warm-up catch along the first-base line, people a little curious about what's going on, feeling the eyes on us.

A father and son run out toward right field, the dad with a ball and glove and the boy with his slightly undersized bat, not the standard Little League aluminum bat that the other kids have, that sends a ringing noise through the air, but a wooden bat, a Louisville Slugger tee-ball bat. I see him now, holding that bat, trotting out along the chalk line behind his dad, a jaunty step, he's proud of his dad, who looks like a real athlete, like he could have played two sports in college, he's looking around to see if the other kids are looking at him, but he's also a kid and he's taking it in, looking at the grass, squinting up at the sun, at the sky, stunned by the fullness of the day. Trying to absorb it all, hoping maybe time will stop right this instant, forever, and never start again. That this will be it, right here, on this field, that's all. I see myself at seventeen, already feeling nostalgia for being a kid his age, feeling the weight of all the bright Saturdays I spent in the dank garage instead of in this bath of sunlight and heat and blue and green, embarrassed for how little I had lived, how little my father had lived, wondering if it was something I would pass on to my son. This was the big day for my dad and I had woken up that morning amazed at the rarity of a day like today, when we might come home champs, when we (my dad, me, our family) might get a win for once, but now, standing here looking at all of this, I remember how stupid I felt as I realized that for most of these kids, a day like this happened every weekend, that none of these kids thought of life that way, as a series of mostly bummer days with the occasional chance at getting a win *against life*. Who thinks that way? I was seventeen. Who thinks that way at seventeen?

They set up about fifty feet away from each other, two endpoints of a little father–son axis, and the dad began lobbing slow overhand pitches to his son, and the boy would swing at them, hitting about one out of every six or seven, weak little grounders that dribbled back to his dad, that his dad would run up to and field as if they were hard hit, which made his son feel a little better, but also a lot worse. The kid was small, and I had been a small kid, and I remember what it was like. He looked like he was getting frustrated. He didn't have any bat speed, even for a kid his age. The bat was probably about three ounces too heavy.

But then, after about three dozen pitches and four or five dinky glancing hits, the kid got ahold of one. The sound it made. It was a perfect sound. Crack. Clean off the sweet spot. Even as he was hitting it, I don't think he believed it was happening. I remember thinking how much I wanted that to be my father–son axis, how bad I wanted to be the one hitting that ball.

The kid's dad whipped his head around, as did all of the other kids, and their dads, and even the director. Everyone stopped and turned and watched the ball fly over his dad's head and then over the grass of the adjoining field, and then over the infield, and land, right on home plate of the other diamond. The kid had arms like wet noodles, didn't even really have shoulders yet. It had to have been 250 feet. I saw it happen and I'm seeing it again now and I still don't believe it happened.

The only person who hadn't watched it was my dad. I didn't know that then, but now, I see that. He just stands there, looking at our sad prototype, holding a vacuum tube in one hand and his other hand on his head, and looking like he knows it just slipped away. The director turns back from watching the kid, which was just the break he needed to stop my dad's awkward fumbling with the machine. There was a mumbled half apology about needing to get back to the office for a meeting, and a promise of perhaps continuing this at a later date which I now see as a courteous refusal of the director to acknowledge what had happened, but even then I knew, given me, given our family, that this was it, that there wouldn't be another chance, that this was the high point of our arc and from here, we were heading into unknown territory.

The fallout started the next morning. It must have taken a night for it to process, a few hours spent alone, stewing over it, replaying the memory over and over in his head, asking what if. It must have taken that time for the damage to register on his ego, on his shell, on his sense of purpose and navigation, on his physical body, even. He didn't get out of bed until ten, which was very late for him, about four and a half hours late for a Sunday morning, and when I saw him he looked sore, like he'd aged years in one night. My mother went to temple early and I was left in the house to wonder when he would get up and what it would be like when he did. He went into the bathroom and after a long shower and a long period of silence before and after, he emerged from there and walked into the kitchen just after noon. He didn't look at me, didn't ask where Mom was. We sat and ate noodles that she had cooked and left on the stove. He heated his up and then picked at them looking mildly repulsed. I asked him if he wanted me to heat up some soup. He didn't answer. After he ate, he put his plate in the sink and I heard him go down into the garage and I was thinking, just for a second, what if, and I was about to go join him when I heard the garage open and his car rumble out the driveway. He didn't come back until after I'd gone to sleep that night, and the next day, he went to work and we never talked about that day again.

(module δ)

conjectures, currently unproven but believed to be true

That a moment has a thickness to it, a size.

That a moment is measurable. That there will be a finite number of moments in the history of the universe.

That there is no unique global time.

That chronodiegetics is a theory of the past tense, a theory of regret. That it is fundamentally a theory of limitations.

26

TAMMY makes a face at me I haven't seen before.

"What is that?" I say.

"I don't know. Your dad, I don't know."

"More complicated than I remember. Whatever. Let's keep moving."

"What are you even going to say? If you find him, what will you say?"

After the day at the park, the drifting got worse. It had started years earlier, when I was in seventh grade, or maybe it was the summer before seventh grade, at first just a few seconds at a time, hard to say if my mother even noticed, but before long it was impossible not to notice. By the time I entered high school, my father was regularly drifting five minutes into the past, and when he did that, none of us could talk to him. Well, we could, but he'd never hear us. He would say things to us, transmit the words into the viscous medium of our kitchen, and we wouldn't get the message right away, it took a while for the words and sound to reach us through the light and air thick with delay, with silence and tension, the air resistant to communication and understanding. And then we would answer, but he was already gone, had already moved on, out, away from us. We would try to answer, make meaning from these conversations, these bits of days, these bits of daily life being all we had by then, my mother and I, all we had left with him. We were losing him.

His invention may have been a failure, but his idea wasn't. As it turned out, and I wouldn't find this out until much later, there were twin projects. The director of the institute had already gone to visit another inventor, not far from our town, actually about half an hour away on the peninsula, where sometimes my mom and I would go have a picnic if my dad was working on the weekend. The houses there had Spanish tile roofs and mail-boxes with roofs, too, and little doors, and the driveways were circular, for receiving guests, I guess, and there was a small park that overlooked the ocean, and a swing set and even a cast-iron jungle gym, shaped like a rocket, for kids to crawl up into, a set of bent metal rods, curved perfectly and painted red and white and blue. This other inventor had had a very similar idea to my father's, the differences being mostly in execution, and the only real difference being that, on the day of his visit, his idea worked. That day in the park was my father's chance, our chance to be a part of it, but the director already had seen that the idea could work and didn't need to find a second diamond in the rough. That part of it would have hurt my father, I know, to know that it was possible for someone like him, a talented amateur, out in the sticks, a moonlighting cubicle worker, a wage-earner-by-day, inventor-by-night, to make it. It would have killed him to know that someone had done it, that all his work had been correct, all the work that he had dumped, a week after that day in the park, all the notebooks, in pieces, scattered and scribbled over hundreds of pages, on scraps, on Post-it notes, on index cards, in margins of books, on backs of envelopes taped and folded and crumpled and uncrumpled and crumpled again. It would have killed him to know that it hadn't been impossible, our dream, but that we got one chance only, just once in a lifetime, and we had lost it. And with that, our idea, our prototype was the one lost to history. My father would forever be the guy who did not get the credit, the one swallowed up, enveloped by obscurity, swept away and lost in time.

If I could tell him just one thing, wherever he is, pass him one message, it would be this: he had something. Something to his thoughts, his ideas, the papers in his notebooks, the work we did in the garage. Beyond just a purity to his ideas, a sincerity to his belief, a genuine curiosity, a determination that, if he just sat there long enough, thought hard enough, failed enough times, he'd find a way in. His idea was good enough, would have been good enough for the director, for the world, good enough to be a serious contribution to the field of fictional science, good enough for me, but I don't know where he is, and I have never been able to tell him this.

Here in the garage, where I watched him while he worked, twisting this, tightening that, and realized, not that I didn't know it, but saw more clearly that, fundamentally, my father is, was, has always been a sad man. Sadness was the driver, the motor of his invention, the engine of his creativity. The sadness was generational, accumulated like heavy elements in us, like we were large sea life, enormous ocean fish, swimming silent, collecting the sadness and moving through the deep with it, never stopping, always increasing the quantity in our bodies, always moving forward, never fully sleeping, eaters of sadness. Bite by bite, meal by meal, becoming made of sadness. Passed down like an inheritance, a negative inheritance, a long line of poor, clever men, growing, over time, slightly less poor, and slightly more clever, but never wise.

I remember one late-December morning in my father's study, one of the last days of the year, felt like it was the end of something more. Not the best year, the family had seen better. Overnight the rain and winds had washed the sky and world of all haze and the early-morning light was even, perfect, the light of an artist's studio. I was nine years old and my mother had told me to ask my father to come have breakfast. The clock in the kitchen was ticking. It was a blue plastic circle with a white face, and standard black arrows pointing to hours and minutes and a thin red needle for the second hand, which made discrete movements, jumped from mark to mark in its circumnavigation, with a kind of abrupt yet soft bouncing motion, and a sound that always seemed louder than it should have been.

I called to my father a few times and, not hearing any response, walked down the hall, afraid of what I might find, not hearing a sound, and then, as I approached, I heard a muffled noise, a sound I was certain I had never heard before, and as I peeked in through the mostly closed door of his small office, I saw, for the first time in my life, my father's eyes red and cheeks and chin wet with tears. He was looking at a picture of my grandfather, the one I never met, who died when I was six months old, who died on a different continent, an ocean away, poor and broken and missing his oldest son. I stood there in the hall, a few feet outside the threshold of my father's private study, watching him, looking at him framed by the door, while he looked at his own father, framed in the picture, the three of us, son, father, and grandfather, forming a melancholy axis, forming a chain, a regress, a bridge into the past.

TAMMY makes her face pretty and blows me a kiss on the cheek. Movie-star face, I call it. She hardly ever does it, and only if I'm being nice.

"What was that for?"

"I don't know. For being that kid."

The weeks passed and the months passed. The prototype sat in the garage. He'd moved it to the corner after we got back that afternoon, and covered it with a sheet. He and my mother started to fight more. My father continued to do his own research, on questions that got more and more specialized, and continued to publish his results in journals with titles more and more obscure. No one noticed anyway. That was the worst part: he understood that something was happening, that he was missing the big picture, even as he couldn't grasp exactly what it was or how or why. By the time I was twenty, a couple of years into college, I could already see him the way others did, I could switch between modes of viewing, sometimes as his son, other times not as his son but instead as someone looking at a prideful, intelligent, increasingly self-isolated man. A man drifting slowly into the past.

Then one day, he is back. It is a little more than three years after that day in the park. I hear him in the garage for hours, and into the night, and then every day for six weeks, the testing getting louder and louder. He is working on something else.

Not a time machine. Something darker, more powerful. Science fiction, but not any kind I know of. He never asks me to come down there, never hints at what he is doing, although I know now that he was building the machine that would take him to that temple, and ultimately to wherever he is now.

In the garage, just where we had once built something together, now he is alone, building a different kind of box, one that will carry him away from us, from here, from this life.

27

TAMMY's crying again.

"Well that was a bummer," I say.

"I thought we were supposed to feel better after that," she says. "Learn something about him."

"I did," I say. "I understand that he left us. I understand about how much he cared for us, and it wasn't that much apparently."

I ask TAMMY what would it even mean? To find my father at this point, what would that mean?

Assume a Desired Event EV_f (son finds father).

CHRONODIEGETIC SPACE

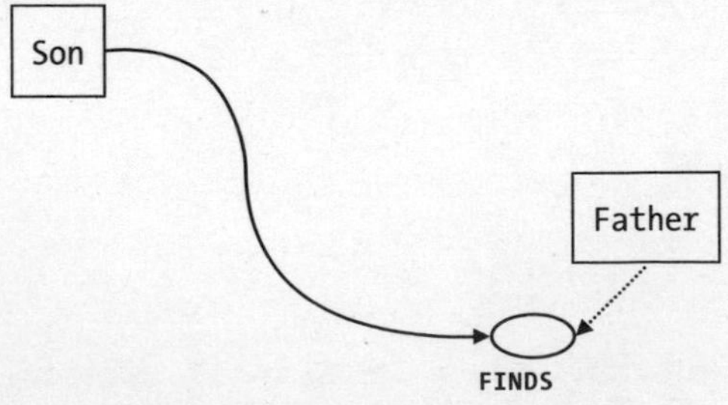

There are two predicates (Son, Father) but neither one is the crucial assumption. The questionable piece of this picture is the operator "finds."

Running that through the Symbolic Operator, we find that *finds* means at least the following: eye contact, discomfort, silence, at least one true thing said, at least one false thing said, at least one overly dramatic and egregiously, recklessly hurtful thing said, and some sort of closed boundary, partial or full, on the emotional asymptote toward parabolic melancholy.

The odds of such a finding occurring are, based on assumptions of the length of a life, the coefficient of conversational friction, the tensile strength of the father–son dynamical social-psychological fabric, and the size of the window of comprehension and dramatic coherence, approximately one time per seventy-eight point three years, subjectively experienced.

A life is about twenty-five thousand days, and a finding occurs about once every twenty-five thousand days.

In other words, once in a lifetime.

In other other words, there is a single day, a single conversation, a single moment in my father's life that I need to find. One time in all of our times together when I can make contact with him, on our divergent, discursive, wandering paths through memory, past tense, narration, and meditation.

Time travel was supposed to be fun, it was supposed to be about going to places and having a bunch of adventures. Not hovering over scenes from your own life as a detached observer. Not just lurching around from moment to random moment, and never even learning about those moments.

And now we're faced with a new problem: we are running out of book. Which is to say, we're running out of fuel. This loop has a preset length. It already happened, and it happened the way it happened, and any moment now, I'm going to find myself going back to Hangar 157 to get myself shot in the stomach.

"That's it," TAMMY says.

I say, What's it.

"When you shot yourself in the stomach, he was trying to tell you something."

It's all in the book. The book is the key.

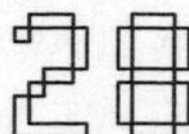

TAMMY opens the panel and the TOAD pops out, and I see on the display that the story is still tracking, has been all along. Through the chronodiegetical principle of past tense/memory equivalence, we've been generating the narration of the text by traveling through these memories.

"Okay, hmmm," I say. "It's still just a book."

Or maybe it's not. I pull the book out of its encasement and, instead of trying to flip ahead (I learned that lesson the hard way), I feel around the edges, not sure exactly for what yet, but, aha, there it is, some kind of groove cut into the pages near the back of the book. I flip it open to find, at the bottom of page 201, a pocket, a little embedded envelope, like this:

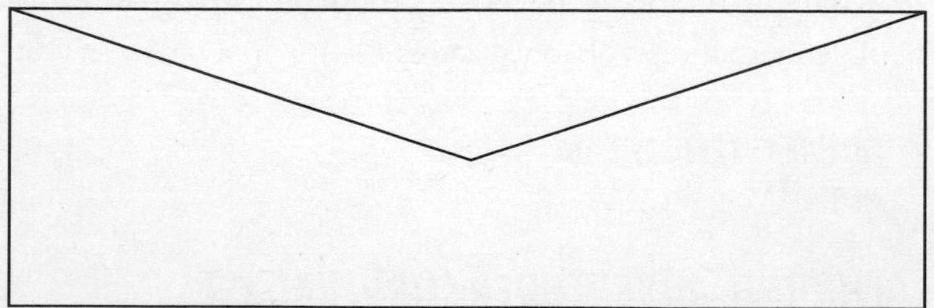

I flip it open and pull out a key, just like I said, the book is the key, which I am grateful to have, even if it does seem a bit literal.

"A key!" TAMMY says.

"Nothing gets past you," I say. The question is, a key for what?

Ed sighs and bites at his left haunch. He can hear in my tone when I'm being mean to TAMMY, and it's his way of disapproving. I pat his head to get him to stop, then notice that he's not biting his haunch, he's gnawing on the box my mom gave me.

"Ed, you're a genius," TAMMY says. I don't disagree.

The box has no seams or folds, was seemingly wrapped by some sort of magical elf, so I have to use a letter opener to stab at it a few times before getting a corner to tear off and because the paper keeps tearing off in bits, it's slow going at first, but then, as I'm unwrapping it, the shape and size and font of the partially uncovered lettering starts to remind me of something from a long time ago, and at the point I realize what that is, I am, for a moment, ten years old again, and my ten-year-old heart starts pounding like a jackhammer in my thirty-year-old body.

There is just enough room in here for me to lay out all the items from the kit, as best I can, on the flat surface of TAMMY's main console.

The lettering on the box top is just how I imagined it looked from the ad in the back of the comic book, slightly fuzzy red-orange block letters, all-caps, blazoned across the top in a sans serif font:

FUTURE ENTERPRISES INC
presents

CHRONO-ADVENTURER SURVIVAL KIT

I set the box top off to the side, facing up, and check off the items one by one against the picture on the box. There's the plastic knife and the Chrono-Adventurer patch, just as I remember, and a map of the terrain and a decoder that is a pair of concentric cardboard disks fastened together concentrically, so that the disks can be turned around relative to each other inside their plastic casing such that if the larger circle, with the encrypted letter, is lined up with the smaller circle, with the decoded letter, a secret message can be sent or translated to a fellow Chrono-Adventurer in the field. There's also a lot of filler, items that, not surprisingly, weren't advertised, like an eraserless No. 4 pencil (labeled SPACE PENCIL), and a protractor (labeled MOON APPROACH ANGLE TRIGONOMETRIC DEVICE), and a little notepad with five sheets of paper, which apparently counts as five items toward the total, cheats, really, cheap items that a ten-year-old me would have found half lame and half still-pretty-cool and possibly endowed with some kind of secret technological features just by virtue of their inclusion in the kit.

I count all seventeen items, look at them spread out, separate from one another, just objects lying there. A bit of a letdown from what I'd hoped for, but then again, I am thirty years old. My father was such a practical man, and this kit no doubt seemed silly to him, which makes the fact that he bought it mean that much more to me. Laid out like this, the contents of the kit remind me of times in our garage laboratory workshop, our version of the director's fancy research institute on the hill, our makeshift center for father–son studies filled with dollar items from the plastic bins at the hardware store. Maybe this is what he wanted me to see. Maybe looking at these items himself, he came to some kind of acceptance himself of why we never made it, the destined-to-fail nature of our little future enterprise. Still, it's hard to believe that he got this kit just so I might someday think back about our work together.

I look inside the empty box and notice something I hadn't seen before. What I had thought was a cardboard structure to hold the packed items in place is really a little box within the box, a compartment someone had built into the box, with a keyhole on the side.

"The key from the book!" I exclaim, like a boy detective.

"Nothing gets past you," TAMMY says.

"I don't remember you downloading the sarcasm upgrade."

"There are a lot of things you don't know about me," she says, and I feel like a jerk, because it's true.

"Well, are you just going to stand there until it's time to go back and get shot in the stomach, or are you going to stick that key in there?"

29

The key fits, thank goodness, because otherwise I'd have been all out of ideas, and I open up the secret compartment to find the eighteenth item.

"What is it?" TAMMY asks.

"A diorama."

It's a little scene, in three dimensions, a miniature version of our family kitchen. He'd taken care to make it proportionally correct. Not only were the height and length of the room to scale, but the depth as well, and it was that third dimension that brought it to life, made the illusion complete. The whole kitchen could fit in the palm of my hand, but it seemed that no important detail was missing. For dinner plates he'd used circles of paper, collected from inside the three-hole punch, glued onto tiny pieces of card stock and then affixed to the miniature kitchen table. There was a miniature refrigerator, and even a miniature calendar, a word-of-the-day calendar with a new science term each day. He hadn't re-created the word of the day, which would have been too small to read, but he had made a little date, April 14. I remember the year we had that calendar I was in fifth grade, which was 1986.

He hadn't made people, too difficult, and maybe that was the point. We weren't there anymore, in the room where we spent all those nights, quiet, tense dinners, the occasional good nights when my parents would tease each other, which always made me feel awkward, and weird, the scene of so many of their epic screaming matches. The kitchen is empty, had been for some time.

"Look," TAMMY says. "The clock."

Inside the miniature kitchen, my father had built a tiny replica of the blue circular clock that hung above the door to the backyard. A tiny working clock. It had an hour hand and a minute hand and a ticking second hand, just like the one we had at home. At that moment, in the diorama kitchen, the time was seven fourteen and about twenty seconds.

The calendar. The working clock. My father is sending a message. He's telling me where he is.

"TAMMY," I say, just starting to feel it, some kind of answer, like a cracked egg, slowly spreading on the top of my head and dripping down all sides of my face. Is this why I'm in the loop? Was it a coincidence that I spent almost a decade drifting, with no tense, with no clock, and the very next day after reentering the world, I got trapped in a time loop? Was it a coincidence that this message from my father, in the form of a miniature kitchen scene, was delivered to me on that very same day?

"TAMMY," I say again.

"I get it," she says.

How many times have I gone around this loop, refusing to move forward? How much of my life have I spent cycling through these events, trying to learn from them, attempting to decipher the meaning of this tableau in front of me, this cross section of our kitchen in that house, this little model of this room in our home, the site of all of those good times and not-so-good times. What is this called, what I am doing, to myself, to my life, this wallowing, this pondering, this rolling over and over in the same places of my memory, wearing them thin, wearing them out? Why don't I ever learn? Why don't I ever do anything different?

Do I always open the package too late?

Is the loop always the same?

Will I ever figure it out in time, early enough to actually do something about it?

Of course I do. Of course it is. Of course I won't.

"We have to go there. Now."

I say this to TAMMY, trying to sound as authoritative as I can, but I already know the answers to my questions, already know what she's going to tell me.

"I wish we could," she says, sounding really bummed, "but the fact is, we didn't."

I look up from the diorama and see what she means. We're circling over the present moment in Hangar 157, banking our descent into eleven forty-seven a.m., where another me, earlier-me, is waiting his turn to do this, to do all of this, all over again.

(module ε)

theorems, miscellaneous

At some point in your life, this statement will be true: Tomorrow you will lose everything forever.

30

When it happens, this is what happens: I shoot myself.

He's waiting for me. Down there. The man who is going to kill me. The man I once was.

I know it happens, already happened to me, and yet, somehow, I have to stop it. I know, I know, I can't. But it's different when it's happening to you.

We're in the approach.

TAMMY arranges her pixels into a sad-faced clock.

11:46:00.

I have one minute left.

Feels like a month, maybe, but if you told me it was less, I'd believe you, and if you told me it was more, I would believe that, too.

I ask TAMMY to calculate the diameter of our path.

"I'm sorry?" she says, and I say I'm sorry, too, for everything and for not being better to her and all that good stuff. The fact that I'm in my last minute of life is making me mushy.

"No," she says. "Not I'm sorry like I'm always sorry. I'm sorry as in I don't understand your question."

"Let me rephrase that," I say. "Objectively speaking, how long were we in the loop?"

"I'm afraid I still don't know what you mean."

TAMMY makes a confused-face clock.

11:46:20.

"What is your problem?" I say. "It's a simple question. How long has it been since we left?"

"The answer to the question of how long it has been since we left," she says, "is that we haven't left yet."

"Oh my God," I say. "You're right."

"You shot yourself, and then you jumped into the machine at eleven forty-seven a.m. that day. From there, you tried to skip ahead, go into the future, but when you did that, you encountered nothingness. There was no future. You hadn't been there yet. And you still haven't. Instead, you got shunted off into that temple, which is completely outside of time, and then your zombie mom gave you the creeps and you spazzed out."

"I didn't spaz out."

"You did, and then you got shuttled back into time, into the father–son memory axis. Which is the past. Which means."

"Which means."

"Which means."

"Which means what?"

"Sorry, I had too many programs running. Which means that, from the point in time at which you shot yourself, you haven't actually ever moved forward. Not one second. Not one moment."

Holy Mother of Ursula K. Le Guin. She's right again.

"But I've aged, haven't I? Haven't I? Don't I have some way of proving it? Five o'clock shadow?" I inspect my face in the mirror.

"Have you eaten anything since jumping in here?"

I think about this for a second. "I guess not," I say. "But wait, aha. I've talked to people!"

"Yeah? So?"

"So talking takes time."

"Who have you talked to?"

"My zombie mom."

"Not a real person. Also, exists on a plane outside of temporal existence."

"Shuttle guy."

"Doesn't exist in time."

"My dad."

"Those were memories. Not events. Also, that's the past. We're trying to figure out if you've moved at all into the future."

Right. Hmm.

"I've been jabbering away with you."

"I'm a computer program. We talk fast. Plus, more important, you talked to me inside this TM-Thirty-one. Which we've already established never moved forward in time after eleven forty-seven."

"I talked to Phil."

"Also a computer program. And again, you talked to him while inside this box."

"It seems you've got an answer for everything."

"It seems I do," she says, sounding a little sad about it, although I can't figure out why just yet.

"Aha," I say. "But what about the book?"

"You mean the magical book that you somehow read and write and it transcribes what you say and think and read all at the same time, seamlessly switching among modes? The book that mysteriously records the output of your consciousness on a real-time basis? That book?"

"Well, when you say it like that, it does sound kind of out there."

"I'm not saying it doesn't exist. It does. I'm just saying, what am I saying? Oh yeah, sorry, I'm a little scatterbrained this morning. Here, let me prove it to you. Open the book up now."

I open it.

from *How to Live Safely in a Science Fictional Universe*

Time travel

1. Any journey in which the interval of *time experienced* by the traveler is not equal to the interval of *time measurable* by those not traveling with them.

2. Chronodiegetical movement that creates a nontrivial, nonsemantic differential between the inner, personal time of the traveler, and the conventional time as agreed upon by the world-at-large.

"See that? See how the little squib there just coincidentally happens to thematically match what we're talking about now? Don't you think that's weird? The book, just like the concept of the 'present,' is a fiction. Which isn't to say it's not real. It's as real as anything else in this science fictional universe. As real as you are. It's a staircase in a house built by the construction firm of Escher and Sons. It's fiction, not engineering. It's a self-voiding fiction, an impossible object and yet, there it is: the object. The book. You. Here it is. Here you are. They are both perfectly valid ideas, necessary, even, to solve the problem your human brain has to solve: how to determine which events occur in what order? How to organize the data of the world into a sequence that appeals to your intuitions about causality? How to order the thin slices of your life so that they appear to mean something? You're looking out a window, a little porthole in fact, just like the one on the side of this time machine you're in, and out your window you see a little piece of the landscape, and you have to somehow extrapolate from that what the terrain of your life is like. Your brain has to trick itself in order to live in time. Which is great, which is necessary, but the flip side of that is, see how long I've been talking? It's been more than forty seconds, hasn't it? And yet it hasn't."

She makes her face into a clock.

11:46:55.

11:46:56.

It comes down to this: three choices.

Option number one: I could stay in here. I could change the past. All I would have to do is move that shifter up one notch, put this device back into neutral for one extra second, wait until one moment after my designated arrival time. I'd get out and who knows what would happen. Everything would be different. I will have just missed my self. I could, without incident, just slip out of this universe and into the next, just like the girl in Chinatown wanted to do. Escape my life. But that would mean not moving forward. That would mean giving up on my father, leaving him trapped, wherever he is.

Option number two: I can keep on doing things just as I have been, let myself be tugged onward by the pull of narrational gravity, the circular path of my own toroidal vector field. Nothing would be easier than to stay the course, this course of minimal action, moving right down the path of least resistance. Would that be so bad?

And then there's the third choice. I could get out of this machine and face what is coming. Instead of just passively allowing the events of my life to continue to happen to me, I could see what it might be like to be the main character in my own story. The event: I have to confront myself. The truth: it is going to be painful. It will end in death, for me, it will not change anything. These are the givens. These are the received truths. I can go through the motions of being myself, ceding responsibility for my actions to fate, to my personal historical record, to what I know is already going to happen. My arms and legs will not change in their movements. I can't change any of that. Nor can I change the path of my body, the words from my lips, not even the focus of my eyes. I have no control over any of it. What I do have control over is my own intention. In the space between free will and determinism are these imperceptible gaps, these lacunae, the volitional interstices, the holes and the nodes, the material and the aether, the something and nothing that, at once, separate and bind the moments together, the story together, my actions together, and it's in these gaps, in these pauses where the fictional science breaks down, where neither the science nor the fiction can penetrate, where the fiction that we call the present moment exists.

This, then, is my choice:

I can allow the events of my life to happen to me.

Or I can take those very same actions and make them my own. I can live in my own present, risk failure, be assured of failure.

From the outside, these two choices would look identical. Would *be* identical, in fact. Either way, my life will turn out the same. Either way, there will come a time when I will lose everything. The difference is, I can choose to do that, I can choose to live that way, to live on purpose, live with intention.

11:46:57.

11:46:58.

"I had it backward," I say.

TAMMY lets out a confirmatory beep. Very official-sounding. And then she makes a blue kind of face at me.

"Yeah." She sighs.

"This whole time I'd thought that my father was the key to my escape from the loop. That he would save me, he would be the answer, when in fact, the answer all along was not an answer but a choice. If I want to find him, then I need to leave this loop. If I want to see him again, I have to get out of this box."

"You realize that you can't do or say anything different," she says. "Or else you enter a new timeline. You have to do what you have to do."

"I know."

"You're going to get shot in the stomach," she reminds me.

"I know."

Now she makes her pixels into a lovely and soft and slightly knowing face. Part sad, and part I-thought-this-day-would-never-come. *It's about time,* she seems to be saying. It's a side of TAMMY I've never seen before, and for a moment I understand that there are parts to TAMMY I've never activated, modules I've never engaged, questions I've never asked and answers I therefore have not received. I never even knew how to use her correctly. I wasted her capabilities.

"So, well, uh, yeah, I don't know how to say this—" I manage to get that far before TAMMY starts to lose it. I've said it before and I'll say it again. You haven't experienced awkwardness until you've seen a three-million-dollar piece of software cry.

I should have been nicer to her. I was pretty nice, though. Nice. What is that? Nice. That's just not enough. I should have taken care of her. I should have taken better care of everyone, of my mom, my dad, my self, even Linus. Even lost girls in Chinatown.

TAMMY has been more than the operating system for my recreational device. She has been, for all these years, my brain, my memory, running all of life's functions for me. Kept me alive. Like a better half. Like the better part of me. She took care of me. Unconditionally. Now I get it. She was, in her own way, The Woman I Never Married, the woman waiting for me if I'd been good enough to deserve her. She was my conscience, she kept me honest about what I was doing in here, or not doing in here.

"I've got to go," I say.

"I understand. I'm happy for you."

"You know," I start to say.

"Yes?" she says, with an eagerness that, for once, she doesn't bother to mask with any kind of simulated emotion face.

"Oh God, what am I trying to say? I, uh."

"Don't say it," she says.

"Okay I won't."

"Yeah, don't."

"I won't."

"Probably a good idea."

"Please say it. Wait, don't."

"Okay fine, I'll say it. There was something, wasn't there? Between us?"

"Yeah," TAMMY says. "Something."

It's silent for a moment.

"Though I have to tell you," she says, "I do have a user-input-based dynamic feedback loop personality generation system."

"So what you're saying is I've been having a relationship with myself."

"To some extent, yes."

"Gross."

"In any event, it's not like it could have ever, you know, worked," TAMMY says. "I don't have a module for this emotion. Whatever it is."

"Neither do I. Whatever it is."

"Yeah. I know," she says, and winks at me.

I want to hug her or kiss the screen or run my hands through her deep, rich, pixilated hair, or something, but pretty much every option seems completely ridiculous. Ed sighs at the two of us, like, *Oh, get a room,* and we snap out of it.

"Well, I guess I'll power down now. Save energy for the approach," TAMMY says, but really it's just to give me a moment alone, a brief interval of quiet to consider what's about to happen to me.

TAMMY closes her eyes, then shuts herself down, a ghostly afterburn lingering for a bit, a transient image of her face persisting there. Her pixels have, to a small degree, permanently lost their ability to return to their relaxed state, leaving, frozen into the screen, a kind of history, a sum total of her expressions fixed into a retained outline, a tracing, an integral, the melancholy algorithm of her soul averaged and captured and recorded as a function of time.

And now I'm alone in this thing.

11:46:59.

This has been the longest forty seconds of my life.

We're in the final approach. The TM-31 lowers itself into the present moment, which starts to come into view. Through the porthole, I can see my past self running toward me, holding his dog under one arm, and a familiar-looking brown-paper-wrapped parcel in the other.

decoherence and wave function collapse

In Minor Universe 31, quantum decoherence occurs when a chronodiegetic system interacts with its environment in a thermodynamically irreversible way, preventing different elements in the quantum superposition of the system + environment's wave function from interfering with one another.

A total superposition of the universal wave function still occurs, but its ultimate fate remains an interpretational issue.

One potential structure that can occur in a closed time-like curve, or CTC, is a worldline that is not continuously joined to any earlier regions of space–time, i.e., events that, in a sense, have no causes. In the standard account of causality required by a chronodiegetical determinist, each four-dimensional box has, immediately preceding it, another four-dimensional box that serves as the emotional and physical cause. However, in a CTC, this notion of causality has no explanatory power, due to the fact that an event can be concurrent with its own cause, could be thought of as perhaps even causing itself. Research in this area is currently the most promising avenue toward the Holy Grail of fictional science—the Grand Unified Theory of Chronodiegetic Forces—a governing law that would serve as a common root for the disparate forces that operate in the axes of past, alternate present, and future, or more formally, the matrix operators of regret, counterfactual, and anxiety.

31

I get out of the time machine.

I'm reminded of the toll-free number I used to call as a kid. I'd call it over and over, trying to set my watch to the minute, exactly, right on the dot, but really, I think I just liked the sound of that prerecorded voice, the lady in the phone, her careful pronunciation of each syllable.

At the tone, the time will be e-le-ven for-ty se-ven and ze-ro se-conds.

How can I change the past? I can't. He's got the gun pointed at my stomach. He looks scared. I don't blame him. I remember being in his shoes, some time ago, a moment ago, I recall what it was like to stare at the future, so full of terror, so incomprehensible, so strange, even when it looks just like you thought it would. Maybe especially so.

His finger is on the trigger, and the trigger is moving ever so slightly backward. How do you convince someone to change, to stop being afraid of himself? How do you convince yourself not to be so scared all the time?

We're both standing here, the same guy on opposite ends of a moment, feeling the same thing about each other, a mixture of self-loathing and self-wonder, that mixture of ever-fluctuating concentration, that interior sludge of volatile fluid running through the pipes of the septic system known as my self-consciousness, that fluid that courses through the conduits of the deep, gurgling plumbing in my head, through which also flows my inner monologue, that running story that I've been telling myself ever since the moment I learned to talk, since before that, even, since I learned to think, the story I began to tell while still in diapers, in the crib, the babbling commentary—sometimes audible, sometimes not—that accelerated into childhood, and then beyond, became a tortured and anguished story in puberty, this decades-spanning confabulation that has continued up until today, up until this very moment, this monologue of my life that will keep running and running and running until it gets cut off, abruptly, at the moment of my death, which could be any second now, because man, does that trigger finger look twitchy. All of that self-storytelling just comes down to this, the most simple of all simple situations. The story of a man trying to figure out what he knows, teetering on the edge of yes or no, of risk or safety, whether it is worth it or not to go on, to carry on, into the breach of each successive moment. It's a survival story, too, the story I have been telling myself. Is he friend or foe, this strange person in front of me, enemy or ally, only, in this case, both sides, all sides, they all happen to be the same person, and that person is me, and the answer, in all cases, appears to be foe. I am my own most dangerous enemy. I know what he's thinking. He's thinking about his training, which says to run, and his instinct, which says to kill, and I know what is going through his head, know that his brain is trying to get him to just slow the hell down and get a handle on all this craziness. I can see the look he's got in his eye, like *Who is this guy? What does he want?* I can see how he is looking right at me, just like I looked at my own future self when I went through this. He's looking and feeling, and what he's feeling is the involuntary shudder, the creeping gooseflesh of dread that comes only at a moment of real self-recognition, self-confrontation, comes only with the genuine possibility of self-annihilation. He's looking, but not seeing, and in between the two, there it is, a gap, and in that gap is my only chance, the only possible margin in which I can change that which cannot be changed. Because he is already looking, his eyes are on me, so it is in his mind that I have to make the change, not a physical change, not one of vision or field of vision, but one of perception. Not what I see, but how I see it. I have to get him to see, see what he's looking at, see me, himself, both of us, see what I'm seeing, which is what he's seeing as well. If only we could both see from the other's perspective, as well as our own, at the same time. If we could do that, then we would have it all, the past and the future, fused, combined into one perspective, we would see the present moment, how it divides us, like mirror images around a temporal axis. If instead of looking forward or back, we could do the opposite, if we could see from the outside looking in, from all sides, if we could only look inward, into the black box of Right Now, if I could get him to do that, he would understand, he would know what I know, which is that it's not necessarily going to be okay, in fact, it probably won't. If I can convince him to do that, then he would know what I know, and then I would have what he has, which is the freedom to act, the chance to do something different, to exert my own will, to not be afraid to let myself move forward into the next moment. I would have what he has, which is the possibility of not doing what I have done countless times, just continuing on in my own time loop. I would have what he has, which is the possibility of moving on. All of which is just dandy and fuzzy and self-affirming, except that none of it solves the problem, which is that I am still the asshole who shot my self the first time around, which is to say, I'll always be the asshole who shoots my self, or to put it another way, he's about to shoot me and there's nothing I can do about it because there's nothing I did do about it.

How many times have I failed before? How many times have I stood here like this, in front of my own image, in front of my own person, trying to convince him not to be scared, to go on, to get out of this rut? How many times before I finally convince myself, how many private, erasable deaths will I need to die, how many self-murders is it going to take, how many times will I have to destroy myself before I learn, before I understand?

TAMMY was right. I can't say anything different or do anything different, or else I end up in a different universe, one that might look just like this one, but one where I don't have all of those memories, one where I haven't figured out where to find my dad, and I can't take that chance. So what do I say? The only thing I can say. What I have already said, the thing that makes the most sense. The truth.

"It's all in the book," I say.

We're two sides of an infinitesimally thin coin. Slice the coin thinner and thinner, and we get closer and closer to each other. We can slice it arbitrarily thin, let the limit of the thickness approach zero. Slice it until there's no one or nothing in between, until we meet at zero. I am an epsilon–delta proof, I am the limit of my own past self as he approaches arbitrarily close to my own future self. We've lived a whole month in that machine, in an instant, a life of memories. We can live our whole lives at zero. For any given epsilon, there exists a delta such that I can come arbitrarily close to shooting myself, and yet never actually do it. I am my own limit, and that limit is the present.

"The book is the key," I say, finishing my argument, hoping it's enough, knowing I can't say anything else.

The words are still coming out of my mouth, the sound is still in the air, the last syllables hanging out there between us, and for a moment, for the longest second in my life, we're frozen, looking at each other. He's trying to figure out what I know that he doesn't know, and what I know is that I don't know anything. I don't know anything he doesn't already know. It's all in there, inside him, waiting to be remembered. Nothing has changed since I got into that machine, an instant ago. I have visited memories, I have explored what never was but should have been, I have gone in a loop, but that loop, like the book, is just another way of expressing the present moment. The loop is a string, looped around and back through, and then drawn tight, into a knot, into a single point, the knot of the present moment. It collapses onto itself, like the present, which only appears when you think about it, like the text of the book. I can't change the past, but I can change the present. How can I convince him of this without actually saying it, only thinking it, only knowing it? But now I see the two of us moving closer and closer, and I see that at the moment I understand it, he does, too, we're both on the verge of it, and so by the time I finish my sentence, he sees, and I see. He knows and I know and he knows I know, and I know he knows.

I reach out and put my hand on the barrel. He lowers the gun.

I exhale in relief. It's over.

. . .

Then: pain.

Because, well, there's no getting around it. I shot myself the first time, which is every time, which is the only time, which is this time. I'm feeling pain because he lowered the gun, just like I did, and he still pulled the trigger, just like I did, and oh my Lord this hurts. Hoo hoo boy, does it hurt, it hurts it hurts it hurts, but I'll get over it, and the important thing is everything that happened, that happens, happens just right. He shoots me and the wave function collapses, all of this rejoins itself, and in a sense, one of us dies, and in a sense, we both do, and in a sense, neither of us does.

When it happens, what happens is a weird guy in a hangar firing a gun at his own stomach, and then jumping into his time machine and opening a box and staring at its contents, some kind of toy, some kind of miniature world that apparently fascinates him, that apparently holds some kind of answer for him, and in jumping into the machine, the guy bangs his leg pretty hard, shattering it, and of course there is the matter of his massive intestinal bleeding from the self-inflicted gunshot wound, and he's lying in there bleeding with a shattered fibula, and the facility-wide alarm systems are going off, all stations alert, and the cops coming to arrest the guy, and then later release him when they realize he'd just returned the day before from over nine years out in the field, and was apparently suffering from exhaustion after spending all that time, a third of his life, in a space the size of a closet, and of course, that's what externally happens, and that is what happens, but it's also not all that happens. What happens is that weird guy mumbling something to himself about the collapsing, infinitely divisible nature of each moment. Above him, the guy can see the massive free-floating clock, the tangible representation of time, he can see it ticking forward. A zero changes to a one, one second slams into the next. 11:47:01. Time to move on. What happens is the weird guy's eyes going all watery, and his dog looking pretty worried, and then the guy's sort of hugging himself, and then he's opening a box wrapped in brown parcel paper, like it's a present, like the weird guy is ten again and it's his birthday, and he's opening a gift from his father, and in a way he sort of is.

I lurch forward and fall, awkwardly, into my time machine. I have always admired protagonists who fall gracefully when they get shot by laser guns or other weapons, and I've always promised myself that if I ever got lucky enough to get into a story where I get shot I would try my best to look cool while my body reacts to the physical blast of the weapon, I would try to do one of those dramatic slo-mo falls, drawing it out, like a choreographed, single-direction dance through space, set to music, with the report of the gun still reverberating through the sound track, but I have to say, when you get shot, it is not the first thing on your mind to fall awesomely. I don't fall even a little cool. I just kind of trip myself and sort of accidentally run into my time machine, in the process slamming my shin against the hatch door about as hard as I remember doing the first time.

When it happens, this is what happens: I still shoot myself. When it happens, I still jump into my time machine, and the memories come flooding back and I still open that package and find what I'm looking for. The moment of all of this is the moment I open that package, and now I understand that what's happened, that's all that's happened, that's why it happens today. I still get shot in the stomach, but as it turns out I don't die from it after all. It all works out just right, and it turns out that you can get shot in the stomach and live, if you do it just right, and it turns out that I'm okay, it just happens to be the most excruciating pain I have ever felt in my entire life, and it feels really good.

APPENDIX A

HOW TO LIVE SAFELY IN A SCIENCE FICTIONAL UNIVERSE

Look in the box. Inside it, there's another box. Look in that box and find another one. And then another one, until you get to the last one. The smallest one. Open that box. See the kitchen, see the clock. Get inside a time machine. Go get your dad. When you get there, he will say, hey. You can say hey. Or you can say, hey Dad. Or you can say, I missed you, you old man. And he is old. Notice how old he is, but don't make him feel bad about it. He's been waiting here for you for a long time, in this kitchen, trapped. Listen to him explain how he never meant to leave. He did leave, though. What he means, and listen to him good, is that he left and by the time he figured out he wanted to come home, it was too late. His time machine broke down, and he got trapped in the past. Tell him you understand. That's what happens to all of us, you should say. The path of a man's life is straight, straight, straight, until the moment when it isn't anymore, and after that it begins to meander around aimlessly, and then get tangled, and then at some point the path gets so confusing that the man's ability to move around in time, his device for conveyance, his memory of what he loves, the engine that moves him forward, it can break, and he can get permanently stuck in his own history. When he says this, you just nod. You are angry, there is still a lot to explain, there are still many questions to be answered, but there will be time for that. Just nod, and be sympathetic, because you should be. You know all about tangled loops yourself now. You don't want to waste any more of the time you have together, because he looks tired. He spent all these years stuck here, waiting inside an empty minute, a safe minute when he knows he can't be found, hoping you got the message. And you did. But he doesn't get those years back, and he's older than you remember. Invite him into your machine. Try not to chuckle as he looks small and impressed and like a boy, marveling at how far things have come. Introduce him to TIM, the operating system in your new machine. Don't tell him about TAMMY. Keep that one for yourself. It was a lovely thing, you and her, but you hope her next operator treats her better than you did. Introduce your father to your dog, Ed, who used to not exist, but now exists again because, hey what do you know, you are kind of a protagonist after all, and protagonists need sidekicks, and he's your trusty sidekick. Make a note to call your boss, Phil, even though he doesn't have feelings. Make things right. Make a note to make a lot of things right. Get back in the box. Set it for home, present day. Go see your mom. Bring your dad. Have dinner, the three of you. Go find The Woman You Never Married and see if she might want to be The Woman You Are Going To Marry Someday. Step out of this box. Pop open the hatch. The forces within the chronohydraulic air lock will equalize. Step out into the world of time and risk and loss again. Move forward, into the empty plane. Find the book you wrote, and read it until the end, but don't turn the last page yet, keep stalling, see how long you can keep expanding the infinitely expandable moment. Enjoy the elastic present, which can accommodate as little or as much as you want to put in there. Stretch it out, live inside of it.

[this page intentionally left blank]

ACKNOWLEDGMENTS

Thanks are not enough but I offer them anyway for now, in lieu of a drink:

To Gary Heidt, all anyone could ask for in an agent. Your creativity keeps me going. I would have given up a long time ago if not for you. It would be nice to actually meet you in person one day.

To Tim O'Connell, my editor at Pantheon, for about one hundred thirty-one different things. I showed you an area in the ground; you showed me where the book was buried. Then you took it out of the ground, dusted it off, and handed it to me. Then you explained what I was supposed to do with it. Basically, you did all the hard work.

To Josefine Kals, my publicist at Pantheon. We just started working together when I wrote this, but my future self says it's going to be awesome.

I am also very grateful to:

Marty Asher, for his invaluable insight, help, and guidance, as well as Andy Hughes, for his production vision and helping to make the Book from Nowhere a reality.

As well as Dan Frank, Patricia Johnson, Chris Gillespie, Edward Kastenmeier, Marci Lewis, John Gall, Wesley Gott, Altie Karper, Catherine Courtade, Kathleen Fridella, Florence Lui, Jeff Alexander, Zack Wagman, Danny Yanez, Harriett Alida Lye, W. M. Akers, Peter Mendelsund, Joshua Raab, and all the others at Vintage/Anchor, Pantheon, and the Knopf Doubleday Publishing Group who have lent their wizardry and wisdom to the making of this book. In the U.K. universe, Nicolas Cheetham, Rina Gill, Becci Sharpe, and Adam Simpson at Corvus have created an alternate and equal version of the TM-31. It is a privilege and an education to work with so many gifted people.

And to Richard Powers, Leslie Shipman, Harold Augenbraum, and the National Book Foundation for encouragement that is difficult to overstate. This weird, mumbly guy scribbles alone under a damp rock, and then, out of nowhere, people like you notice him? Still unbelievable to me, and it always will be.

And I must not forget to thank:

Val Jue, for the gifts of time and peace of mind, Robert Jue for computer expertise, and Rose Lowe. Also, Howard Sanders, Sarah Shepard, Tyler Johnson, the Taiwanese United Fund, and Taiwanese American Citizens League for enthusiasm and support.

Admiration for and apologies to:

Douglas Hofstadter for *Gödel, Escher, Bach,* a book I will never get over, and never stop reading.

And to David Deutsch, for writing *The Fabric of Reality*, a book so fascinating that the only way I could even attempt to get over it was to write a novel based on a complete misunderstanding of your ideas.

I wish I had:

A time machine while writing these acknowledgments so I could go into the future and see who else is going to help make this into a book. I'm sorry I can't thank you by name, but please accept my categorical gratitude, all you wonderful future-people.

Finally:

To Kelvin, for always being so good to me, and for teaching me new things about stories. To Sophia, for reminding me how to enjoy a story. To Dylan, for being a great sleeper and a great guy all-around. To Mochi, for your sad-eyed company. To my father, Jin Yu, a very good engineer and an even better dad, and my mother, Betty Yu, for her inventiveness and fire. And to Michelle, for always being the best version of yourself, even when I'm my worst.

A NOTE ABOUT THE AUTHOR

Charles Yu received the National Book Foundation's 5 Under 35 Award for his story collection *Third Class Superhero*, and he has also received the Sherwood Anderson Fiction Award. His work has been published in the *Harvard Review*, *The Gettysburg Review*, *Alaska Quarterly Review*, *Mississippi Review*, *Mid-American Review*, and elsewhere. This is his first novel. He lives in Los Angeles with his wife, Michelle, and their two children.

A NOTE ON THE TYPE

This book is set in Spectrum, the last of three Monotype typefaces designed by the distinguished Dutch typographer Jan van Krimpen (1892–1958) in 1956.

Composed by Scribe, Inc., Philadelphia, Pennsylvania

Printed and Bound by WorldColor, Fairfield, Pennsylvania

Designed by Wesley Gott